Bonebinder

Peter J Murray

Bonebreaker

Peter J murray

Hodder
Children's
Books

a division of Hachette Children's Books

I dedicate this book to my good friend Trevor Wilson.
His total belief and commitment to my work are
a constant inspiration towards success.

WWW.PETERJMURRAY.COM

Copyright © 2006 Peter Murray
Illustrations © 2006 Simon Murray

First published in Great Britain in 2006 by Hodder Children's Books

A Catalogue record for this book is available from the British Library

ISBN-10: 0 340 91120 4
ISBN-13: 9780340911204

Typeset in Perpetua by Avon DataSet Ltd, Bidford on Avon, Warwickshire

Printed and bound in Great Britain by Bookmarque Ltd, Croydon, Surrey

The paper and board used in this paperback by Hodder Children's Books are
natural recyclable products made from wood grown in sustainable forests.
The manufacturing processes conform to the environmental regulations of
the country of origin.

Hodder Children's Books
a division of Hachette Children's Books
338 Euston Road
London NW1 3BH

Acknowledgement

I wish to offer my sincere thanks to the Yorvik Viking Centre, in particular to Professor Richard Hall, Jane Stockdale, Chris Tuckley and Zoe Durrant-Walker for all their help and support in helping me add authenticity to the historical nature of this text.

Prologue

The Reeds of the Fen

The reeds of the fen
They whisper their tales
Of the warrior boat
With the blood-red sails
Of fighting men
Haggard and wild
Of the Viking man
And the Saxon child

The reeds of the fen
They hardly dare talk
Of the Demon Giant
His penance to stalk
The desolate marshes
Haunting the dyke
Till the small boy comes
His vengeance to strike

The reeds of the fen
They reach to the skies
And pray that the clouds
Will hear their cries
That Good will conquer
And free this land
From the evil that stalks it
The Bonebreaker Man . . .

PJM

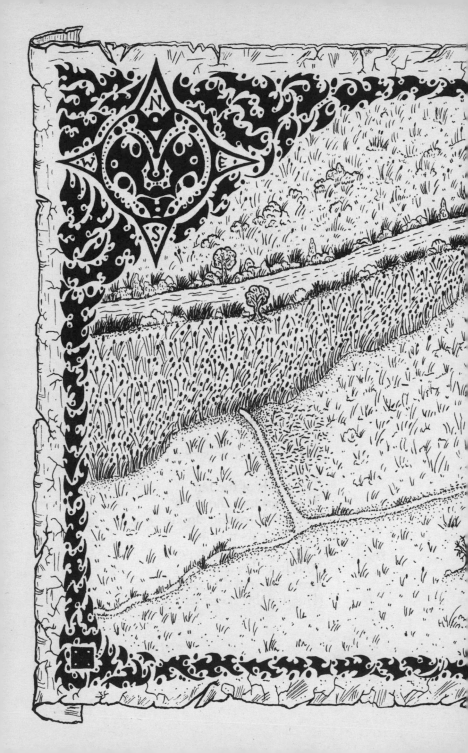

Fenthorpe

AD 865

1
Wilfrid the Invincible

Wilfrid stood as still as a heron, his spear poised above his head, its point angled down towards the gently gliding current. His legs tingled in the coolness of the stream as he watched for the first signs of his prey.

A voice, full of excitement, sounded from upstream, *'I can see them, Wilfrid. Masses of them! They're heading straight towards you!'*

Wilfrid tensed and stared intently down into the clear water, watching the long trails of waterweed swaying between his legs.

A small dark shape shot downstream just by his right knee, but Wilfrid didn't move a muscle. A second shape quickly followed, this time darting by his left knee. A third swam straight between his legs.

And then there were flitting shapes everywhere, all

swimming frantically downstream. Now the water turned black – the shoal had arrived. But still Wilfrid never moved. To the fleeing creatures he had become part of the river, another natural obstacle in their bid for freedom, from the terror that pursued them – and it was this that Wilfrid was waiting for.

'*He's here, Wilfrid, and he's huge – a real monster!*'

Wilfrid felt a tinge of nervousness as the last of the small fish shot past him. He tightened his grip on the shaft of the spear and stared down towards the water.

His eyes bulged in awe as the huge black shape drifted into view.

The great fish stopped a short distance in front of him. At the same time, the sun peeped from behind a cloud and a shaft of sunlight lit up the fearsome predator with dramatic effect.

Now Wilfrid saw his adversary in all its monstrous beauty.

Its head was almost as big as his own, with intense black eyes staring upwards. The great protruding jaws, slightly open, revealed rows of needle-sharp teeth. A camouflage pattern of olive-green spots sparkled along its flanks, the long back topped with a bright-orange dorsal fin. The body was perfectly streamlined, capable of thrusting itself forward with enormous power.

For the next few seconds, which seemed like an eternity, Wilfrid stared down at the fish and the fish stared back – two warriors sizing each other up.

Like all Saxon hunters, Wilfrid knew only too well that water played strange tricks and that it was necessary to aim the tip of his spear slightly upstream of the fish's head. Taking a deep breath, he brought his arm down with lightning speed and felt a solid resistance as the surface of the water erupted.

'*By thunder, Wilfrid . . . You've hit him!*'

Wilfrid didn't have time to reply.

Despite being speared, the fish turned and bolted upstream, catching him off balance. Wilfrid's world turned upside down and became a whirling mass of pebbles, sand and bubbles. But despite being dragged headfirst into the riverbed, he refused to let go of the spear. He rolled over and over and his head struck a rock, but he still refused to let go. Finally, just as he felt his lungs were about to burst, another hand grabbed on to the spear shaft and helped him back to his feet.

A moment later, the two Saxon boys stood midstream, wrestling with the weakening fish, shrieking and shouting as the battle drew to a glorious close.

They had won!

Wilfrid had won!

A boy had succeeded where every man in the village had failed. This fish had always evaded capture . . . until now.

Wilfrid the Brave!

Wilfrid the Invincible!

Wilfrid – the proudest Saxon boy in all the land!

* * *

The two hunters carried their prize into the village – Wilfrid at the front, Dunstan at the back, the speared fish hanging from the shaft supported across their shoulders. It was a fantastic procession and the villagers gasped in disbelief.

'Mercy upon us! How did you manage that, young Wilfrid?' one of the elder men asked with a shocked expression.

'I helped him!' Dunstan stated proudly.

'Well ... just a bit!' Wilfrid added, looking serious.

The two boys walked on. 'Just wait until your mother sees this – er . . . I mean . . . *finds out* what you've done. She'll be speechless,' Dunstan beamed.

Wilfrid smiled to himself.

They neared the familiar woven hut and saw the old woman sat by the entrance. She was grinding some grain in a big stone bowl and, as they approached, she looked up and smiled. 'Good Mother Earth! That fish will feed the whole village for a week. It's bigger than you, Wilfrid.'

'But not as big as his heart!' another voice sounded from the doorway.

Wilfrid looked across at his mother. She stared above him, her sightless eyes giving her a ghostly appearance.

'Do you know what this is, Mother?'

She continued to stare into space, her nose twitching. 'It's a fish . . . and I'm guessing it's the grandfather of the river – or at least it was, until it tangled with my fine son. And you, Dunstan – no doubt you had a hand in its downfall?'

The two boys lowered the great fish to the ground. 'Yes I did, Bethan. In fact, were it not for me, I'm sure Wilfrid would have drowned.'

Wilfrid swung round and turned on his friend, grabbing him in a headlock and wrestling him to the ground. 'It's not true, Mother. I could have done it all by myself.'

The old woman got to her feet and split the two boys up. Bethan laughed from her place in the doorway. A young child's cry sounded from somewhere behind her.

'Matilda is awake. I'll have to tend to her. Should we invite everyone to the gathering place for supper? Will there be enough to go round?'

'I think there's enough fish in that carcass to feed the entire village,' the old woman laughed. 'I'll give the two hunters a hand to prepare it, Bethan.'

'And when we've eaten, will you tell us what you know, Mother — around the fire?' Wilfrid asked in an excited voice.

'Perhaps,' she replied quietly.

'And will you tell us what you know of the giant warrior?' Dunstan asked, getting back to his feet and dusting himself down.

Bethan's expression changed. She looked troubled. Without speaking, she turned and went inside the hut to attend to her young daughter.

At the same time, the old woman left her stone bowl and muttered something under her breath. She, too, seemed anxious as she led the two boys away to begin the job of preparing the once-mighty fish for a feast everyone would remember.

Though the singing had stopped, the gathering place at the centre of the village buzzed with excited chatter. The flames of the fire had died down and the smell of cooked fish drifted from its glowing embers through the cool evening air.

Looking up at the clear starlit sky, and then at the smiling faces surrounding him, Wilfrid glowed with pride. He was so pleased with himself – to think that he alone (well, Dunstan just a little bit) was responsible for this magnificent feast ... It was the best day of his life!

Wilfrid's mum sat by his side, his sister, Matilda, cradled in her arms.

'Come out and sit before us, Bethan!' someone shouted. 'It's time to tell us what you know!'

Bethan frowned and rocked her daughter in her arms. 'Well, just for a few minutes . . . Matilda is tired and wants to sleep.'

Wilfrid watched as his mother rose to her feet and allowed the old woman to guide her through the crowd to a wooden seat by the fire. When she was safely in position the crowd went silent. They waited patiently as she angled her head up towards the night sky and concentrated hard.

A woman, surrounded by young children, suddenly

shouted out, 'Tell me, Bethan – will I have any more offspring?'

Wilfrid watched as his mother turned her head in the direction of the caller. 'You will have four more, Ymma . . . two boys and twin girls.'

'Mercy upon us!' the woman shrieked back. 'I'll die of exhaustion!'

Everyone laughed and Wilfrid beamed. He felt proud of his mother, sitting there, the centre of attention. As well as being an excellent storyteller, she had always been able to predict the future with a good deal of accuracy, and most of those in the village believed firmly in her powers – none more so than her son. But then Wilfrid noticed that his mother wasn't joining in with the laughter . . . She looked worried – tense.

She answered a few more questions, and then someone suggested she told a few short stories to the younger children sat by her feet.

'I've heard it said that there is a giant warrior – the one they call the Bonebreaker?' Dunstan blurted out.

The entire crowd went silent. Bethan lowered her head and said nothing.

It was one of the men drinking on the edge of the gathering place that spoke first: 'It's just a myth – a stupid story. The warrior doesn't exist!'

Bethan looked towards the young man and her face took on a twisted expression. 'You're a fool, Edward. He's as real as the Viking who killed my husband. Don't doubt it for a second!'

The young man wobbled a little — he'd had far too much to drink — and then he shouted back: 'Your husband was killed a long way from here . . . Some say he was heading for York — took money to spill Viking blood and it cost him his own blood in the end. And that's as much as anyone knows. The rest is all hearsay. If you ask me the stories of giant raiders from the North are all blown up and rumour.'

'Well, no one is asking you,' a woman in the crowd snapped back at him. 'And you should listen to Bethan — she's usually right!'

'That's just the point. She's not *always* right — and in this case—'

'Oh shut up, Edward!' another woman interrupted. 'Go back to your drink and let Bethan speak.'

The young man sat down — almost fell down. The other men gathered around him and joined in with his sarcastic laughter.

Wilfrid looked across at them and frowned.

Edward was a stout, muscular man and most of the men in the village looked up to him; but as Wilfrid's mother had always said, 'Edward is big in body but small in mind'.

Bethan rose to her feet and prepared to move off. 'It's best I stop now . . . I don't want to frighten the children. I need to get Matilda to her bed. I must meet with the elders on the morrow.'

Wilfrid jumped to his feet. 'Don't worry yourself, Mother. We're not frightened. If you know something of the giant, we all want to know.'

A ripple of excitement spread through the crowd, especially from the children.

Wilfrid's mother stared with white sightless eyes across the sea of heads in front of her. Her complexion glowed eerily in the dying firelight and her voice suddenly took on a haunting tone: '*Very well . . . I'll tell you what I have foreseen. But believe me, when I've finished, nobody will sleep easily in their beds tonight!*'

2
Nightmare Predictions

'I have had this dream so many times – and again last night . . .'

The entire crowd had lapsed into complete silence. Even the dogs, curled up by the fire, had cocked their ears, as if they too wanted to listen to what Bethan had to say.

'In this dream I'm a bird, soaring through a blackened sky over the sea far below. And I can see the boats beneath me – longboats cutting through the waves . . .'

'Viking boats!' somebody in the audience shouted out.

The blind woman went on, her voice beginning to tremble a little, 'From the North . . . seven of them – always seven! And as I swoop down I can see their brightly-patterned sails billowing in the wind.'

'Is *he* among them – the giant warrior?' Dunstan asked from Wilfrid's side.

But Bethan didn't hear. She was in some sort of trance, her head craned upwards towards the stars – looking without seeing . . . seeing without looking . . . reliving her dream in vivid detail.

'The sails of the seventh boat . . . are different.'

A young girl grew restless by her feet. 'Why are they different?'

'They are blood-red – some say stained with the blood of *his* victims.'

A gasp befell the crowd and Wilfrid felt his heart begin to race in expectation.

'And then I soar upwards, high above the fleet, watching the raiders steer their vessels towards the shore. One by one their great boats arrive, filled with warriors. I see them wading through the shallow surf . . . up on to the beach . . . standing in a long line stretching across the sand . . . waiting for the final boat to arrive.'

'*His* boat!' someone uttered in a frightened tone.

'As this last boat grinds upon the shingle, a score of men leap out and scatter away, glad to be out of his reach – *for even his own live in fear of him.*'

The speaker paused – the nightmare becoming real in her head. The audience seemed frozen, as if everyone had stopped breathing – hardly daring to hear what would follow . . .

'And then, as *he* steps out . . . once more I find myself swooping downwards.'

Again, a gasp echoed around the crowd as someone shouted

impatiently, 'And what do you see, Bethan? Please tell us.'

'I see a man twice the size of any other. He is truly a Goliath, his shoulders broader than two oaks and his limbs thicker than a horse's neck.'

Wilfrid sat transfixed whilst his mother continued to share her vision.

'As I spiral downwards, I see the fearsome helmet — fashioned out of iron, adorned with four bronzed panels. I can see the letter "S" stamped between the eye sockets, which are hollowed and black — as if no human eyes exist behind the mask.'

The young girl who had grown fidgety by Bethan's feet began to cry. Her mother picked her up and moved away. A few more mothers seized the opportunity to collect their children and do the same.

'This is scary,' Dunstan whispered across to Wilfrid.

Wilfrid looked back with a serious expression. 'And it's not just a scary story. This is true. If my mother dreams it, then it will happen.'

After the mothers and young children had departed, the crowd resettled.

Bethan, who had never moved a muscle, continued to describe her awful vision: 'As the long line of warriors ready themselves, they stand restless, waving their swords above their heads and shouting their praises to their god, Odin — until their leader takes a step forward and raises a giant hand. Now they become still . . . silent. A Viking puts a war horn

17

to his lips and it sends out a mournful sound – a sound from the very depths of Hades – and it signals the Bonebreaker to charge forward with his warriors in his wake. I can feel the ground trembling beneath his feet. I can hear his heavy breathing, smell his foul breath, and see the spittle falling from his fearsome mouthpiece.'

At these words, Wilfrid found himself beginning to panic – not just for himself, but also for his mother. He stood up, weaved his way through the seated crowd and shouted at her, breaking her trance and bringing her back to the present. 'Why are you so close to him, Mother?'

The crowd held its breath in anticipation of the soothsayer's reply.

'In these dreams I see through the eyes of the bird who perches on his shoulder: the great raven who searches out his master's victims – a creature sent straight from the underworld. And I know that it is only a matter of time before this harbinger of doom swoops over these cliffs and heralds *his* coming.'

'Oh, good God!' a woman shrieked out from within the crowd. 'Pray tell us when this will happen, Bethan.'

Bethan aimed her sightless eyes towards the speaker and tears began to roll down her cheeks.

'I tell you all seated before me now, that as moon becomes full, the Bonebreaker will step upon this shore and bring death and destruction to our village. Many of us will be killed – some of us taken as slaves.'

An anxious voice sounded from within the crowd: 'But you said I would have four more children. How can that be?'

It was Edward who answered first. 'It's like I said, Bethan doesn't know what she's talking about,' he sneered.

Bethan ignored him. 'It's true enough, Ymma. You *will* have four more children, and like you, they will all become slaves to the heathens.'

Another hush fell across the crowd before the women sauntered sadly away. The men stayed on, sitting around in groups, drinking – but Wilfrid noted that even they were subdued and talked in quiet whispers.

Wilfrid and Dunstan sat among the tall reeds, soaking up the heat of the early morning sun.

'Your mother put the fear of God in everyone,' Dunstan said, as he removed the knife from the leather sheath hanging from his waist belt.

Wilfrid lay back with his hands behind his head, staring up at a flock of geese. They formed a perfect 'V' formation as they flew across the marsh. 'I know. I didn't sleep a wink last night,' he replied sleepily. 'What are we going to do?'

Dunstan picked up a piece of twig and began sharpening one of its ends. 'What do you mean?'

'I mean that we've got to do something to protect ourselves – from the Bonebreaker.'

'You have real faith in your mother's powers, don't you? You really believe he's coming here!'

Wilfrid looked at Dunstan, his straight brown hair falling around his freckled face and lying across his broad shoulders. Though he was eleven years old, like Wilfrid, he looked at least two years older. His eyes were wide with excitement.

'Like Mother says, he'll be here when the moon is full,' Wilfrid went on. 'We've got to do something to protect ourselves. We need to make a plan.'

A huge beetle scurried by Wilfrid's feet. All in an instant, Dunstan brought down the sharpened twig and stabbed it cleanly through the back. He lifted the speared insect in triumph as he spoke. 'We'll need help – we can't possibly take him on by ourselves.'

Wilfrid nodded and looked back to the sky. He began to pick out shapes amongst the rolling white clouds. He imagined he saw a horse . . . and then a warrior's face.

'We'll ask Inga.'

Dunstan threw the stick, complete with dead beetle, into the marsh. 'But she's a girl!'

'A strong girl!' Wilfrid added. 'She's as strong as any boy. I've seen her carry two struggling goats at the same time, one under each arm.'

'Well, I know she likes you, Wilfrid. I've seen that look on her face. It wouldn't surprise me if she hasn't got you lined up for a husband.'

Wilfrid felt himself blush and quickly changed the subject. 'Come on – it's time to go.' He climbed to his feet and Dunstan did the same.

'Where to?' Dunstan asked.

Wilfrid ran his hands through his shoulder-length auburn hair and dusted down his light-brown woollen tunic. 'We're going to ask Inga to go down to the beach with us. We'll work out the Bonebreaker's attack route and draw up some sort of defence.'

Dunstan didn't sound too impressed. 'Shouldn't we ask the men in the village to help? Surely we can't do this by ourselves?'

'You heard Edward last night. He doesn't believe in Mother's dreams. And the other men will follow what he says – they always do. In any case, we're not exactly on our own.'

'What do you mean?'

'Mother! She'll help us. We need to ask her every detail about those dreams of hers. And then we'll be one step ahead . . . waiting . . . ready to strike the Bonebreaker before he strikes us!'

As Wilfrid strode out towards the village, he found himself compelled to take one last look up at the deep-blue sky – to see if he could see any more shapes in the rolling clouds. And as he did so, both he and Dunstan heard the screeching cry from high above their heads.

A small black shape wheeled and turned, and both Saxon boys knew at once that this was the great raven, circling and spying . . . the Bonebreaker's bird . . . the creature from Hell!

3
night Watch

The three Saxon children stood side by side on the firm yellow sand, looking out to sea. The blue expanse stretched out before them, small waves rolling in and breaking gently at their feet.

'We'll need a watcher,' Inga said.

Wilfrid turned and looked at her jet-black hair blowing back in the stiffening breeze. 'I'll do it!' he said firmly.

'You can't do it all on your own,' Dunstan spoke up, still gazing out to sea.

Inga adjusted her brooch and tightened the cloak gathered around her shoulders. 'No . . . We must take turns. When should we start?'

'Tonight,' Wilfrid replied. He picked up a pebble and flung it far out into the waves.

Dunstan picked up a pebble twice as big and flung it

twice as far. 'You're right. I'll take first watch.'

'And when they arrive . . . What do we do next – apart from rouse the village?' Inga asked, her voice full of concern.

'We won't be able to do much down here,' Wilfrid answered. 'We need to take full advantage of the cliff tops. Follow me – I've got some ideas.'

They walked up the steep incline to the vantage point at the top of the sandstone cliffs. A large boulder lay by the path.

'Are you thinking what I'm thinking?' Dunstan asked with wide eyes.

'It's much too heavy!' Inga sighed.

'Not if we go about it the right way,' Wilfrid added confidently. 'We need a lever . . .'

Fifteen minutes later, the three friends were swinging together on the end of a long length of washed-up tree trunk. They had wedged the other end under the side of the boulder, a small rock acting as the fulcrum. As they swung up and down, the large boulder rocked precariously on its base.

'Enough, for now!' Wilfrid gasped for breath. 'With a bit more help we can move the rock and send it hurtling down the path.'

Inga looked at him through intense hazel eyes. 'You're clever, Wilfrid. I would never have believed it possible.'

'But in truth,' Dunstan chipped in grumpily, 'even if we

do send the rock hurtling downwards, what's the chance of it striking the Bonebreaker?'

Wilfrid thought he detected a little bit of jealousy in his friend's sulky response. For a long time he had known that Dunstan admired Inga. In fact, Dunstan hero-worshipped her.

'You're right!' Wilfrid answered. 'And that's why we need more than one line of defence. We need to set more traps. Come on!'

For the next few days, Wilfrid, Dunstan and Inga kept themselves busy – always on the outskirts of the village, always involved in some strange activity: digging in the ground . . . hunting for leaves and twigs . . . collecting small stones.

The men of the village laughed when Wilfrid tried to explain that they were preparing to defend themselves against the Bonebreaker's impending attack.

Some of the village elders complained that the three children were shirking their real duties. Inga should be taking her turn at weaving and cooking, and Wilfrid and Dunstan had failed to take their turn at the most hated of all village jobs: taking all the waste to the large rectangular hole by the edge of the village – the foul-smelling cesspit!

Some of the elders complained to the children's parents, but Bethan reacted angrily. Her nostrils flared as she ranted back at them. 'They are right to try to prepare defences, no matter how childlike their plans. And you should be helping them! The children are the only ones listening to me. It seems that neither Edward nor any of the other men are prepared to heed my warnings . . . The day is dawning – and soon it will be too late . . . The Northern raiders may be on the water even as we speak!'

But the elders just grumbled and walked away.

That night, the three Saxon children sat around the fire in Wilfrid's hut. Wilfrid's mother sat with them and spoke in hushed tones.

'You have been busy, my children. It's a pity the other men haven't followed your example.'

'It's so sad, Bethan,' Inga sighed. 'Only the women believe in your powers. The men just scoff.'

Bethan nodded gravely, 'Men are such fools! They rarely use their heads and refuse to see what is so obviously happening around them.'

Wilfrid kicked off his leather shoes and warmed the soles of his feet by the fire. 'What do you mean, Mother? What do you see?'

It seemed a strange question for a child to be asking his blind mother, but Wilfrid knew that she understood.

'Have you not noticed the change in the animals? They are restless and unsettled. The dogs slink around and the cats have all but disappeared. I no longer hear the scurrying of rats and mice – even they have moved away to search out a safe refuge.'

The awestruck faces of the three children glowed in the heat of the dancing firelight. Their crouching shadows flickered around the rough-hewn walls, adding to the eerie atmosphere.

'Are we truly doomed, Bethan?' Dunstan asked.

'I fear the worst,' she replied. 'We can only pray to God. But there is one thing you children must promise me.'

'What is it?'

'In the storage hut there is a deep chamber dug out at its centre.'

'I know – I've seen it,' Dunstan shouted excitedly. 'It's where the ale is kept – it's cool down there. There's a ladder leading down into it.'

'And in its darkest corner you will find a small wooden cover leading down to a deeper pit. It's where the village gold and a few other treasures are stored. It's a perfect hiding place,' the blind woman said quietly. 'And if all goes wrong and the village is plundered, I want you three to hide down there with Matilda and stay there until the heathens are gone. No one will ever find you there. Now, will you promise me?'

'We can all hide down there – you too, Mother,' Wilfrid stated frantically.

'The space is small and a blind woman will always be a hindrance. You children are the only means to our survival. When all this is over you must pick up the pieces and try to rebuild our community. I see all this in my soul – it makes perfect sense. Now will you promise?'

The three children nodded solemnly and retired to their beds deep in thought.

It was only as the last fire in the village finally died out that Dunstan slipped out of his bed and made his way down to the starlit cliff tops.

He was more than glad to take the first watch – there was no way he could ever get to sleep after all that Wilfrid's mother had said.

He looked up at the night sky . . . The moon shone down on him – *it was almost full!*

It was morning when Dunstan's eyes blinked open, trying to cope with the strong sunlight. 'Oh, by thunder – I've slept through. It's hopeless . . . I would never have known . . .'

As confused thoughts raced through his mind, Wilfrid and Inga appeared from the footpath behind. 'Come on, sleepy-head,' Inga teased. 'We know you've been asleep. Some use you are!'

Wilfrid saw the embarrassment in Dunstan's face and felt sorry for him. 'I'm sure Dunstan was awake for most of the night. He probably just dozed in the last hour or so. Anyway, let's go – there's work to do.'

Dunstan looked sheepish and said nothing.

The three friends walked back to the village and headed for the storage hut. There was usually somebody around – checking on the contents or moving stuff in or out – but on this occasion they were lucky: there was no one about.

'Everyone's at breakfast . . . and that's where we should be. We'll have to be quick,' Wilfrid whispered. 'Let's get in and take a look while we've got the chance.'

They sneaked through the entrance and immediately spotted the thatched cover lying on the ground beside some other stored materials.

Wilfrid and Dunstan dragged back the panel, and Inga gazed into the chamber. A small makeshift ladder led down into the darkness.

She climbed down the ladder and the two boys followed.

At the bottom of the pit the air was fusty. They groped around and, as their eyes grew accustomed to the gloom, they saw the stone jars standing in rows.

'Just as I said,' Dunstan proclaimed proudly. 'Jars of ale — they store it down here to keep it cool.'

They groped around further, searching for the cover to the inner pit.

'There's something here, behind this jar.' Wilfrid found himself whispering.

They all crouched down and ran their hands over a small wooden cover. Wilfrid and Dunstan were about to lift it when they heard footsteps from above.

'Quick! Dunstan! Give me a hand!'

Together they reached up and slid the thatched panel back over the top of them. A moment later they were crouching with Inga in the darkness listening to a familiar voice above their heads.

'The women are becoming restless. It's affecting their work. I've not eaten properly for the last few days.'

It was Edward's voice.

A different voice replied, and Wilfrid and Dunstan heard Inga gasp beside them. 'It's Bethan's fault – filling their heads with her stories and tales of woe.'

'It's Father!' Inga whispered. 'He's always been pig-headed!'

'Shush . . . Don't let them hear us,' Wilfrid whispered.

The voice continued. 'Do you think there's any truth in it?'

'There *are* tales of a huge warrior. They say he's not human – more savage than any man could ever be. I've heard it said that a man from over the marsh lost a friend at the back end of the harvest. He was one of many who got all his limbs broken and died in agony.'

'The Bonebreaker?'

'So they say. The village was ruthlessly plundered, and the rest is hearsay – exaggerated rumour, if you ask me!'

Wilfrid felt a shiver run down his spine as the two men's voices trailed away.

'Pig-heads! All of them!' Inga exclaimed as they climbed out from the storage pit.

'Never mind that,' Wilfrid said. 'At least we know this hiding place works. They never even suspected we were down there.'

'But when the raiders come, they'll enter the storage hut, find the pit and then find us,' Inga said.

'Which is why we need to hide in the lower pit.'

Dunstan was the last to climb the ladder back to the surface. 'Well as far as I'm concerned it's only a last resort. I wouldn't really want to be hemmed in down there with the Bonebreaker charging around above us. If he found us we'd be trapped.'

Neither Wilfrid nor Inga could disagree with that.

The three friends went very quiet and slunk back to the centre of the village. To dampen their mood even further, they were immediately seized upon by two of the village elders. They were scolded and given jobs to do. Wilfrid and Dunstan were sent with buckets of waste to the cesspit and Inga was instructed to join the other women in preparing the midday meal.

Wilfrid took the second night watch.

He was sure his mother had heard him sneak out of the hut — she'd often told him her hearing was so strong she could hear a mouse's whiskers bristling — but she'd lain there, hugging Matilda's sleeping body close to her chest, and had said nothing.

He made his way down to the cliffs, constantly looking up at the sky, searching for the moon. But it was cloudy and all he saw was blackness. Perched on top of the cliff by the big boulder, he gazed out to sea . . . but under the dark sky the waves were invisible. Only the roar of the surf kept his senses alert and stopped him falling asleep.

Hour after hour he stared out across the inky-black ocean, looking for any signs of invasion, but there was nothing to see or hear, just the relentless crashing of waves on the shingle below.

Finally, as the dawn light competed with the darkness, the clouds drew back and the moon made a brief appearance. To Wilfrid's horror it was as near full as it could be, just a sliver missing from one side.

He began to shake with nervous excitement and his stomach began to churn. He strained harder to see across to the horizon . . . and thought he saw a light far out on the waves. And then it disappeared . . . and then reappeared.

It was there all right.

And as other lights appeared and disappeared, Wilfrid realised that they were bobbing up and down below the waves. They were boats, with small fires burning on their decks.

A sickly feeling formed in Wilfrid's stomach. He swallowed hard and tried to stay calm. There was no doubt in his mind that these were the dreaded Viking longboats. As he continued to stare out to sea, the dawn began to break and the lights faded. But Wilfrid was sure that he could see a row of black shapes out on the water.

This was it – the Vikings were coming . . .

His mother's nightmare vision was about to come true!

4

Invasion

Wilfrid sprinted back to the village and sneaked into the huts of his two friends. A short while later, the three of them stood on the cliff tops and watched the longboats draw ever closer.

'Just as your mother said – seven of them!' Dunstan quivered.

Wilfrid pointed to the boat on the extreme left. 'And one of them has different colour sails!'

'*Blood-red!*' Inga cried, putting her hands to her face.

Suddenly, all three of them jumped back as a shrill cry sounded from close above their heads. Wilfrid was the first to look up and see the great black bird wheeling and kiting in the rapidly lightening sky. He took a slingshot from his tunic and picked up a small stone from the ground. He took careful aim and then changed his mind – dropped the ammunition back to the ground.

'What's wrong?' Inga and Dunstan asked together.

'My mother . . . in her dream . . . seeing through that creature's eyes – it's like she's inside it!'

'There's no time for dreams!' Inga replied harshly. 'That's no dream out there – *those raiders are real!*'

'We must put our plan into action,' Wilfrid yelled into the strengthening wind. 'Inga – go and alert the village. They'll take more notice of you.'

As Inga sprinted away, Wilfrid and Dunstan watched in horror as the huge longboats approached the shore. It would only be a short time before Vikings were treading on their soil . . .

By the time Inga returned with Edward and her father, the Vikings were rowing through the surf – heavily-clad warriors clambering out into the waves and wading towards the shingle beach. The sound of their deep voices carried in the wind up on to the cliff tops.

'The soothsayer was right!' Edward's voice trailed away. 'We are doomed!'

Inga's father was the next to speak. His voice quaked. 'We must flee for our lives. We cannot possibly face up to them – we're not prepared!'

'It's too late to run!' Inga screamed back at him. 'You should have listened! It's true what the women say – you're all pig-heads!'

Wilfrid looked down as more and more Vikings waded

ashore and assembled themselves into a line stretching across the beach. He estimated that there were already around two hundred warriors – more than double the number of men in the village. 'At least *we've* made a plan,' he stated. 'And it might just give our people more time to make an escape.'

Down on the beach, the line of raiders began to move restlessly, stamping their feet, chanting strange incantations and wielding their swords and axes high above their heads. Inga began to cry and her father put his arms around her.

Then Dunstan let out a chilling cry: 'LOOK! HE'S HERE!'

They all stared down as the last of the longboats beached. The Viking line danced even more excitedly as the gigantic figure clambered out and waded ashore, dwarfing the other warriors around him.

'The rumours are true!' Edward stammered in disbelief. 'He's bigger than two men!'

The distant figure stood on the wet sand, rooted to the spot like a giant oak, a strange layer of vapour clinging to his form. The head was completely hidden by a fearsome helmet, exactly as Wilfrid's mother had described it in her dream. It gave him an alien, inhuman appearance.

Without warning, a screeching cry sounded from somewhere over the cliff tops, and every warrior looked up as the great black bird spiralled downwards.

'That bird again!' Wilfrid muttered. 'I should have killed it when I had chance.'

The raven circled the beach before swooping down and landing on the crest of the Bonebreaker's helmet. The giant warrior roared like a lion and wielded a huge battle-axe high above his head before the bird took off again. It flew straight up the cliff path towards the terrified Saxon onlookers.

Once more, it wheeled close above their heads and screamed its bloodcurdling cry so that every warrior, including the Bonebreaker, looked straight towards them.

Wilfrid felt his heart race as the Bonebreaker stepped forward.

Further down the line, another Viking put a great horn to his lips. It sent out a loud mournful sound that sent a shiver down Wilfrid's spine. The Bonebreaker immediately broke into a trot, taking giant strides towards the cliff path, the other Vikings following quickly.

'MERCY UPON US – THEY'RE COMING!' Edward screamed.

Inga pushed away from her father and rushed towards the boulder. At the same time, Wilfrid and Dunstan dragged the washed-up tree trunk towards it. Within seconds, they were all swinging on the end of the driftwood lever, desperately trying to send the huge mass of sandstone rolling down the incline.

'We're almost there!' Wilfrid yelled. 'Just one more go . . .'

The boulder rocked back and forth, grinding and crunching on its base. Finally, it lunged forward . . . sent up a great cloud of dust . . . *and stopped after two yards!*

Inga screamed in terror: 'THEY'RE HALFWAY UP THE PATH . . . THERE'S NO MORE TIME!'

But Wilfrid was having none of it. 'No! We can still do it! The boulder's ready to roll. If we all push on it . . .'

Inga watched in awe as Wilfrid, Dunstan and the two men ran up to the rock and pushed against it for all they were worth. Wilfrid was right. The boulder had come to rest on a steeper incline, and their combined effort sent it on its downward track.

'YESSSS!' they all screamed together.

They watched in fascination as the boulder rumbled down the path, gathering momentum and hurtling straight towards the charging invaders.

The Bonebreaker was already halfway up the path and was the first to spot it.

He grabbed the nearest Viking, dragged him by the neck to the front and used him like a shield. As he rammed his unfortunate victim hard up against the rock, the man was killed instantly; at the same time, the sandstone mass was deflected over the side of the cliff.

Wilfrid and his onlookers gasped in horror as the Vikings resumed their charge, the Bonebreaker making a chilling roaring sound as he waved his axe high in the air. Wilfrid felt the ground shake beneath the warrior's massive feet and put his fingers to his ears as the great bird hovered above his head, screeching and squawking.

His mother's worst nightmare was coming true . . .

'QUICK! FOLLOW ME!' he yelled at the top of his voice.

Without question, Wilfrid's followers sprinted after him to the top of the cliff. They ran on to the point where the reed-fringed path divided and headed off along the left fork towards the great marsh – in the opposite direction to the village.

Seconds later, a flat carpet of reeds covered the ground in front of them.

'Run to the left of the reeds . . . Don't step on them!' Wilfrid yelled.

Edward and Inga's father did as instructed. Once on the other side of the reed carpet, they ran on along the path until they reached the great marsh and hid amongst the bulrushes.

With racing hearts, they waited and listened as the Bonebreaker and his men advanced from the top of the cliff and reached the fork in the path.

'Will they follow us?' Dunstan asked in a panic-filled voice.

'They have to!' Wilfrid replied. 'We have to lead them away from the village.'

The raven made a beeline for the marsh, hovered above their hiding place and let out another piercing cry.

The Bonebreaker immediately responded and charged along the left fork towards them, two hundred Viking raiders close on his heels.

'The devil-bird has done for us!' Inga's father cried out. 'We have no choice but to fight. Edward and I will try to delay the advance. You three children make your escape.'

'Have faith, Father!' Inga whispered. 'Wilfrid is no fool!'

They crouched low and watched as the Bonebreaker and his army of warriors reached the carpet of reeds.

Once again, the giant halted the advance.

He peered suspiciously at the mat of fallen reed-stems and roared at two Vikings immediately behind him. At first they cowered back, but the Bonebreaker pushed them forward. They stepped on to the reed carpet and prodded cautiously with their spears. Halfway across, they were still feeling solid resistance and becoming more relaxed. The Bonebreaker bellowed at them to move on more quickly. They responded – and a moment later one of the men suddenly felt fresh air as his spear-tip passed through the carpet into a deep hole. His left foot discovered the hole at the same time, and he screamed as his body fell through the reed-stems down on to the protruding spears rising vertically from the pit below.

Inga put her hands to her ears and closed her eyes as the warrior writhed in agony, speared like a hunted boar in the base of their trap.

The Bonebreaker roared in anger and charged to the left

of the trap and on towards the marsh where the fugitives were hiding. Some of the raiders chose to run to the right and immediately found themselves in difficulty as they sank rapidly into the muddy swamp.

'They've run into Madman's Marsh!' Edward whispered excitedly. 'What a stroke of luck!'

Wilfrid watched Inga's angry expression as she turned to Edward. 'That's not luck! This is part of our plan! It's all calculated – worked out! You know, the sort of thing you men should have done!'

They watched as once again the Viking advance slowed to a halt.

Several of the raiding party tried desperately to pull their sinking companions from the lethal swamp, but for some it was too late. They could only gather round and watch as the doomed warriors disappeared beneath the stinking mire . . . Their screams, loud at first, trailed away into hideous gurgling cries.

The devil-bird, still screeching in the misty air above Wilfrid's head, returned to its master and perched on the Bonebreaker's massive shoulders.

'This is incredible!' Dunstan whispered. 'We're really slowing them down, making them think.'

'You're right,' Inga's father added. 'They've lost a good few men already and they still haven't found the village yet. With a bit more luck—'

But before he had the chance to finish, Wilfrid gasped as

the Bonebreaker pointed in the direction of a thin smoke column.

'Great thunder! Some fool's lit a fire!' Wilfrid shrieked.

To make matters worse, an old man, totally disorientated, hobbled out of the reeds straight towards the raiders.

'Oh no!' Edward sighed. 'It's Egric. Why didn't he stay with the others?'

'They'll not harm him, surely?' Dunstan said. 'He's an old man.'

A shiver ran down their spines as the Bonebreaker roared. One of the Vikings immediately ran over, caught Egric by the arm and dragged him towards the giant warrior.

As Egric screamed for mercy, the Bonebreaker took hold of the old man's frail body and hoisted it up above his head – as if in some sort of offering to the gods. With another mighty roar he brought the old man down over his raised knee and snapped his back like a dry twig.

Wilfrid and his band of followers squirmed in terror – even the Bonebreaker's men stepped backwards.

Throwing the lifeless body into the marsh where several of his own men had perished, the huge warrior turned to face the rising smoke column. Wilfrid looked on in horror as the Viking army regrouped and readied to charge.

Once more the Viking horn sent out its melancholy sound.

Bloodcurdling battle cries filled the air as the raiders charged – this time straight towards the village.

'Let us pray that our people have gone into hiding,' Inga sobbed.

As the last of the Vikings disappeared through the reeds, heading towards the smoke column, Wilfrid stood up and moved out from his hiding place.

'B-but what about my mm-mother?' he stammered, tears streaming down his cheeks. 'She has no chance of escape and will be completely at their mercy!'

5
Pillage and Plunder

The raiders stormed into the village, the Bonebreaker leading the charge like a raging bull. Wilfrid's defence party stalked up behind, desperate to do something, but equally determined not to be caught.

Half the village had already begun to flee, raised by the alarm, but many of the older and weaker Saxons were too slow. As the raiders ran among them, ransacked their huts and plundered their belongings, the hapless victims fell to their knees and begged for mercy.

'W-what can we do?' Edward stuttered to Inga's father. 'I feel like a coward crouching here. We should be helping . . . defending our people.'

As he spoke, they looked on and saw three young men race out of a hut and run to face the Viking charge.

'It's Cuthred and his two brothers!' Inga cried out.

They watched in horror as Cuthred, the biggest of the three brothers, raised his sword against the Bonebreaker. The giant took hold of Cuthred's arm with his mighty fist and forced him to the ground. In the same instant he brought down his huge axe and took off the young man's head cleanly with one blow.

Wilfrid felt sick and Inga put her hands over her mouth to stifle her scream.

They watched helplessly as the two other brothers leapt forward, brandishing their weapons — but the Bonebreaker was uncannily fast for his size. Staving their blades off with the shaft of his axe, he knocked them both to the ground. Two other Vikings ran up and held the points of their swords to the men's throats, but the Bonebreaker waved them away. The two brothers dropped their swords, rolled over and tried to crawl away, but the Bonebreaker seized them each by an ankle and held them aloft like two rag-dolls.

The other Vikings roared with laughter as the giant held them up to the sky.

And then, to Wilfrid's horror, the Bonebreaker snapped each of their legs like pieces of dry twig before dropping them on the ground screaming in agony. Finally, he picked up Cuthred's head by its blood-soaked hair and held it up to the sky, roaring like a lion and uttering words that neither Wilfrid nor any of the others understood.

As the two twisted bodies were dragged away, writhing in

pain, Inga's father whispered in a voice trembling with fear, 'These heathens are straight from the Devil.'

'What can we do?' Edward whispered. 'We can't just stay hidden like this.'

'We've got to find my mother,' Wilfrid insisted.

'And what about *my* mother?' Inga asked, turning to her father.

'There's only one thing we can do – pray they'll be spared, taken as prisoners and kept as slaves . . . We can try to rescue them when it gets dark,' Edward said.

'Provided they don't find us in the meantime,' Dunstan quivered.

Wilfrid turned on his haunches and stared at their panic-stricken expressions. 'Follow me – I know one place where they'll never look for us!'

The Vikings ransacked the village with ruthless determination.

The frightened onlookers watched everything from their new hiding place.

They had sneaked around the very edge of the village and crouched behind one of three woven panels hiding the cesspit. Wilfrid had guessed that the Vikings would keep well away – the smell was unbearable!

Inga was still sobbing quietly and Wilfrid and Dunstan were subdued. They had never seen anyone struck down before – let alone someone they knew. The Bonebreaker was still carrying Cuthred's head around . . . And his brothers, Elfgar and Tostig, were probably dead too – butchered by that demon and his vile army!

'Look!' Wilfrid whispered with renewed excitement. 'There's Mother, carrying Matilda, and there's your mother, Inga.'

They watched as the Vikings herded the women into the village centre, pushing and kicking them and generally treating them like animals. Some of the women were set to work to prepare food.

Matilda was crying hysterically and this caused renewed feelings of determination to well up in Wilfrid's stomach. He looked at Dunstan and Inga. 'Thank God they're alive!' he whispered. 'And now *we've* got to stay alive – to fulfil our promise. We've got to get hold of Matilda and hide until they've gone.'

Dunstan and Inga nodded.

Wilfrid looked anxiously around the clearing and across to the storage hut.

The invaders strode around, abusing the survivors and screaming their loud Viking curses. They looted the huts, bringing anything of value back to the stockpile at the centre of the village, every now and then discovering someone in their hiding place – killing them if they were too old, or keeping them for slaves. Animals were slaughtered where they stood – just a few spared and tethered, bound for the Viking longboats.

The smell from the cesspit caused Wilfrid's eyes to water as he spoke: 'The Bonebreaker's disappeared. I'm scared. He might be looking for us.'

'He'll never find us here,' Inga whispered back.

A familiar screech filled their ears. They looked up and saw the giant raven perched on the edge of the panel. It stared down at them with black beady eyes and screeched even louder.

Wilfrid picked up a stone and prepared to throw it – but it was too late.

As the bird took off into the air, a heavy-bladed axe came down and split the panel from top to bottom. They all fell backwards and found themselves looking up at the Bonebreaker.

Edward instinctively took his knife from his leather pouch, jumped up and readied himself to strike. The Bonebreaker roared with laughter. His huge frame made Edward's muscular body seem puny – and Edward's knife seemed inadequate, to say the least.

They all watched as Edward lowered his knife and knelt in front of the giant warrior. 'I don't know if you understand our Saxon tongue, but if you have any feelings I ask you to spare our lives, especially the children. Take us as slaves. We will serve you well.'

Wilfrid knew that Edward had acted wisely. It was the only thing to do. If they were taken prisoner, they could always attempt to escape later. At least they would be alive!

The fearsome helmet angled down towards Edward's pleading expression. Wilfrid wondered if the brain behind those hollowed black eye sockets was capable of pity?

In answer to his question, the Bonebreaker raised his right arm and brought down his fist, like a mighty hammer, crashing on to the top of Edward's head.

There was a sickening crack and Edward fell backwards.

Nobody could be sure whether it was Edward's skull that had split or whether his neck had broken, but he lay quite still, staring up at the cloud-filled sky with lifeless eyes.

Inga screamed. At the same time, her father rushed towards Edward's body. Wilfrid found himself overcome by a sickly feeling. He almost vomited over Dunstan as the two friends clung to each other, shaking in terror.

The Bonebreaker roared instructions and two of his men responded by dragging Edward's corpse away. Several others rounded on Wilfrid and his three companions and took them away to join the prisoners at the centre of the village.

Wilfrid's heart leapt at the sight of the hooded woman, Matilda clinging to her chest. 'Mother . . . I can't believe you're still alive – and Matilda!'

'But I don't know for how long, Wilfrid. They haven't realised I'm blind yet, and a blind woman is of no use to them.'

Wilfrid saw that his mother had covered as much of her face as possible with her hood. He took hold of her hand.

'I can be your eyes, Mother. I'll lead you. And as for any Viking who tries to kill you – he'll have me to deal with first!'

Wilfrid felt his mother's grip tighten as she squeezed his hand affectionately. He looked up at her shadowed features and saw the tears running down her cheeks.

'Only God knows what will become of us, Wilfrid, but remember what I said earlier. You must try to hide, to stay behind – rebuild this community when the heathens are gone.'

'I can't hide now, Mother. I need to be with you and be your eyes. Where you and Matilda go, I go!'

Bethan fell quiet and said nothing else. Wilfrid knew that he had his mother's stubborn determined streak and she knew it too. They would stick together and survive as a family. And then there was Dunstan to think about – his best friend. Dunstan had no family. He'd been found abandoned on the marsh as a baby and brought up by the old woman . . . Her body lay dead by Wilfrid's hut and Dunstan had cried at the sight of it. Wilfrid would have to watch out for his friend from now on.

The Vikings had no wish to stay overnight.

There was a sudden urgency to evacuate the village. Along with the other survivors, Wilfrid, his mother, Dunstan, Inga and her parents were all tied by the waist and strung together in a long line ready to be led down to the beach and herded on to the boats.

'They're keen to catch the tide,' Wilfrid's mother whispered. 'They have to move quickly.'

The Bonebreaker reappeared and the army of raiders rapidly reassembled. Within a short time the long line of prisoners was making its way towards the cliff tops and the steep path descending down to the beach.

Inga's father took the load off Bethan by carrying Matilda. Wilfrid, thankfully, had been tied directly in front of his mother, so that he was able to guide her steps. Dunstan had become separated and was somewhere nearer the front. To add to the air of defeat and uncertainty, the sky went black and it began to pour with rain.

As the procession moved onwards, the rain came in torrents and the pathway quickly became muddy and slippery. All the time the great raven circled overhead. Its screeching cries filled Wilfrid with the most awful sense of foreboding.

As the line began its steep descent to the beach, the rain drove into their faces – and Wilfrid's mother slipped! She almost went over the edge of the cliff, taking Wilfrid and the woman tied behind with her.

Someone screamed and the procession ground to a halt.

Wilfrid felt his stomach tighten as one of the Vikings rushed back to find out what had happened. Bethan pulled her hood tightly over her face. The warrior roared in his own tongue and prodded Wilfrid and his mother with the tip of his spear. And just as Wilfrid thought they had got away with it – *the Bonebreaker appeared!*

His frame was so big that it was difficult for him to stand on the narrow path without forcing everyone else over the side. Wilfrid and the other prisoners felt their hearts begin to race as the great warrior roared and made a grab for Bethan.

He seized her by the neck in one of his powerful hands and her hood fell away from her face. Pulling her closer he stared into the whites of her sightless eyes. Before Wilfrid or anyone else had chance to react, the monster took a huge knife from his waistband, cut the ropes attaching her to the line, and lifted the helpless woman up into the air, holding her at arm's length.

Wilfrid screamed at the heartless warrior: 'LEAVE HER ALONE! PUT HER DOWN!'

The Bonebreaker cast a glance at Wilfrid before raising his mother even higher. Wilfrid and the other prisoners watched helplessly as she gurgled and spluttered for breath, choking in the grip of the Bonebreaker's mighty fist.

Wilfrid slipped his little knife from the pouch on his belt and began cutting the other part of the rope still attaching him to the line. He had to do something!

The Bonebreaker looked to the heavens, the rain driving down into his face, a bolt of lightning suddenly lighting up the blackened sky. As the thunder followed, he gave a mighty roar and threw the blind woman's body back on to the path.

They all watched in horror as one of the other Vikings handed the Bonebreaker his lethal axe. As the giant raised it to deliver the soothsayer the fatal blow, she screamed up at him in a loud voice that seemed almost unnatural – ghostly – as if someone else was speaking through her:

'*BY ALL THE POWER IN MY SOUL, I CURSE YOU, SIGURD. I COMMAND THAT YOUR SPIRIT BE CHAINED TO THESE SAXON MARSHES UNTIL SUCH TIME THAT MY DESCENDANT AVENGES YOUR SINS. ONLY WHEN THE FINAL BATTLE HAS BEEN FOUGHT WILL YOUR EVIL SPIRIT BE FREED FROM PURGATORY.*'

Another flash of lightning added effect to Bethan's words, and then, as a great roar of thunder filled their ears, the Bonebreaker passed his axe back to the Viking by his side.

Just for a moment, Wilfrid thought his mother might be spared – that somehow her curse had had an effect on the heathen standing over her . . . Did he really understand her words?

But then, to everyone's despair, the Bonebreaker grabbed Bethan by the hair, lifted her into the air and cast her over the side of the cliff like a rag-doll.

Wilfrid screamed and gazed down over the edge of the path. A hush fell over the entire procession as everyone, including the giant warrior, peered downwards.

Bethan's mangled body lay spread-eagled across a clump of jagged rocks. She was barely alive, blood spewing from her mouth. She tried to speak. But it was Wilfrid who spoke first.

'Mother! I – I'm coming down! Don't move!' he yelled at her.

The dying woman angled her gaze up at her son's terror-stricken expression. She tried to force a smile . . . took one last gasp of air . . . and died.

Wilfrid fell to his knees and sobbed into his hands. A moment later, he noticed that along with his own people, every Viking, including the Bonebreaker, was staring down in stunned silence at his dead mother.

Her curse had somehow struck home.

She had screamed the name 'Sigurd'. The 'S' on the giant's helmet – she somehow knew his name. This is what had unsettled the raiders.

Wilfrid looked up at the giant by his side – still rooted to the spot, gazing down on his latest victim. He was completely distracted.

Wilfrid knew what he had to do.

Seizing the opportunity, he crept around the back of the line and began sprinting up the slippery path back towards the cliff top. He had to hide, stay behind – rebuild the community, as his mother had instructed.

'WILFRID! NO!' a voice screamed after him.

He didn't turn until he was at the top of the path. And then he looked back and saw Inga and her father waving frantically. 'God be with you!' he shouted down at them. 'My place is here!'

And just before he turned to head for the village, he took

a last look down the line – and heard the screams as both Vikings and prisoners tried to get out of the way of the charging warrior. At least three unfortunates were shoved brutally over the side of the cliff as the Viking leader thundered after him.

It seemed that the Bonebreaker had no intention of allowing Wilfrid to survive!

6
Survival

Wilfrid lay in the blackness, breathing in short gasps.

He sensed the monster stalking him, looking and listening for anything that would betray his presence . . . The devil-bird, perhaps, somewhere close by.

And his intuition was correct!

The Bonebreaker had returned to the village and made a great torch from the dry thatch taken from the underside of one of the hut roofs. He had gone to the gathering place where the great fire had long since died down, dampened by the rain, but the giant had known that the embers would still be smouldering underneath.

And now, with lighted torch, he struggled to tread gently as he searched inside every one of the village's thatched huts. It did not take long – each dwelling place had been stripped bare of its belongings, just a few dead occupants still within.

Every time the Bonebreaker drew a blank he cursed and roared, spat on to the ground, and set fire to the underside of the dwelling roof — conscious that the tide would not wait. And all the time, the raven circled overhead, staring down with beady eyes . . . desperate to find the small boy.

Finally, the demon giant reached the storage hut.

Stooping forward to pass through the doorway, the Bonebreaker saw that the space was completely empty.

Wilfrid lay quite still. He tried to work out how long he'd been hidden. He had to give it a bit longer . . .

The Viking looked down at the floor and saw the woven panel covering the pit. The Bonebreaker knelt to the ground and slid the panel back with one hand whilst wielding his blazing torch in the other.

Wilfrid, beginning to feel faint from lack of oxygen, lay as still as a corpse.

The monstrous warrior ignored the frail ladder and lowered his huge bulk into the rectangular pit, peering into the illuminated space. A noise sounded from a dark corner, and he turned and roared at the same time. But it was only a rat! It ran over his foot and he stamped on it with the other, flattening it to a bloodied pulp and bellowing with rage.

There was no one else in the pit!

The Bonebreaker was furious — he had failed to find the boy.

Wilfrid hardly dared to breathe lest the Bonebreaker was still searching for him.

The Bonebreaker stamped around the base of the pit in anger and his foot struck the small wooden panel. He held his torch over it, stooped down and ripped it away with a powerful hand.

And still Wilfrid lay in his tomb of blackness, wondering how much longer he could survive there, his head swirling into dizziness.

The Bonebreaker dropped to his knees . . . lowered his torch . . . poked his huge head into the inner pit . . . saw a gold crown, a bag of coins and several jars of wine – but no Saxon boy!

In a complete rage, he climbed back to the surface and torched the roof. Like the others, it just smoked and smouldered at first, but finally it became a blazing inferno. Now the entire village was alight.

Taking a last look around, the Bonebreaker roared once more – half in anger, half in triumph – and set off with great strides back towards the beach and his waiting men.

The rain clouds had long since given way to the late-afternoon sun and the fires in the plundered village blazed brightly, immense heat consuming everything remotely flammable.

Only the flooded cesspit remained untouched, a bunch of hollow reeds sprouting from its centre.

Sensing that he was completely alone, Wilfrid sat up and emerged from beneath the stinking mire, casting aside the hollow reeds that had supplied him with life-giving air. He

looked almost as fearsome as the Bonebreaker — a mythical bog-monster in all its grotesque glory!

He ran down to the sea, his feelings spiralling out of control, laughing and crying at the same time. He washed himself free of the stinking waste. He stood and shivered and looked out to the horizon and saw that the fearsome raiders had departed. A great wave of relief flowed through his body, but the feeling was quickly replaced by the horror of all that had happened . . . to his mother . . . and his people.

He longed for everything to return to normal, to be as it had always been — and he cursed the Bonebreaker and his vile army.

The next day, Wilfrid began the grim task of recovering his mother's body. He was determined to bury her with the dignity she deserved, in the burial place above the cliffs. It took all day to do — the work was backbreaking, but Wilfrid's strength and determination helped him to achieve his goal. And when all this was done, he took one last look around the smouldering remains of their community.

As he walked among the carnage, he thought about Dunstan . . . It seemed like only yesterday that they had carried the great pike together, proudly into the village. He thought about Inga — her jet-black hair blowing back in the wind as they'd stood looking out to sea. Wilfrid knew that his two closest friends were strong in body and nature, and that there was a good chance that they would both survive their ordeal. The thought comforted him.

As he walked out of the raised village towards the great marsh, a few of the villagers who had managed to escape were returning. They ran towards him and threw out their arms to greet him. And as Wilfrid approached them, he determined that he would fulfil his promise to his mother – to rebuild their proud Saxon community.

And he would do it!

Wilfrid the Brave!

Wilfrid the Invincible!

Wilfrid – the proudest Saxon boy in all the land!

As for the Bonebreaker . . . Wilfrid knew that his mother would not rest in her grave until justice had been done. She was special and her curse had meant much more than just angry words.

One day, someone in their ancestral line would avenge the great wrong that the Bonebreaker had brought upon their people!

Fenthorpe

AÐ 2006

7
Billy Boy

Billy Hardacre crouched as still as a heron, his clear blue eyes focused firmly on the tip of the little orange float. He felt sure it had trembled, that something beneath the glassy surface of the Forge Pond had disturbed it.

'Wait . . . not yet!' the boy by his side whispered.

Billy stared at the float harder than ever, willing it to disappear. Every muscle in his body tensed, ready to strike.

'BILLY!'

The loud yell from across the field almost gave the two boys a heart attack. At the same time, the little orange tip plunged beneath the mirrored surface.

'Strike!' Calum shouted.

Billy jerked the long fibreglass rod upwards and held his breath in anticipation.

From somewhere behind, a loud yell rang out again: '*BILLY! WHAT DO YOU THINK YOU'RE DOING?*'

Both Billy and Calum ignored the voice. Neither of them looked back as the woman pushed her way through the half-rotten five-bar gate and struggled with her pushchair over the rough ground towards them.

'Yes – I've got one!' Billy shrieked.

'Great! I think it's a small roach,' Calum said enthusiastically. 'Don't lose it. Reel it in quick before it gets off.'

As Mrs Hardacre drew up beside them, breathing hard and looking slightly red in the face, Billy reeled in the line and a small fish skirted across the surface, flashing silver in the weakening sunlight.

'Billy! What do you think you're playing at! It's half-past four! I've been worried out of my wits!'

Billy raised the rod higher so that the little fish became a flying fish. He swung it through the air and caught it in his right hand. He put down the rod and stared at the small creature. 'Sorry, Mum. I only meant to stay for five minutes, but Calum let me have a go and I got sort of – carried away.'

'It's my fault, Mrs Hardacre,' Calum joined in. 'I've been pestering Billy to have a go at fishing since I took it up last Christmas.'

'It's not your fault, Calum,' Mrs Hardacre sighed, lifting Billy's two-year-old sister from her pushchair. 'It's his responsibility to think about these things – he should have either let me know he was going to be late or got himself home at the proper time. Now we'll all be late for our tea and Beth's hungry.'

Billy continued to gaze in awe at the silver fish cradled in the palm of his hands.

Its little eye with a black centre and red outer ring seemed to stare back at him. The silvery body was perfect in every detail; rows and rows of overlapping scales, like chain-mail armour. The fins: blood-red, deep vermilion and perfect in miniature.

The fish suddenly flapped in his hands and, as its mouth opened and closed, gasping for life-giving oxygen, Billy sensed the creature's primeval instinct to survive.

Without warning, his little sister shrieked and pointed at it, snapping him out of his daydream.

'Sorry, Mum. I know I should have come straight home. But fishing – *it's brilliant!* Can I take it up, like Calum?'

'Billy, put the fish back before it dies,' Calum said sternly.

As he crouched down by the edge of the pond and placed the small roach on the surface, Billy's mum, still holding Beth, walked up and leant over. They all watched as it lay there, lifeless.

'No, you can't take up fishing, Billy,' his mum said firmly. 'I can't afford it – and in any case, it seems cruel to me. That fish is dead.'

Billy stared at it glumly. His heart sank. He felt guilty –

like a murderer. How could he have killed such a beautiful creature? His mum was right – fishing *was* cruel.

But as Calum leant forward and ruffled the water with a stick, the little fish stirred to life and swam swiftly away. Billy sighed with relief. Beth shrieked out and pointed again, and even Mrs Hardacre smiled.

'See, Mum – it's not cruel. The fish is OK.'

'That may well be true, Billy. But it doesn't alter the fact that we've got precious little money. Now come on . . . Let's get home for tea.'

Billy wiped the fish slime off his hands with an old piece of towel that Calum had brought along. He reached up and took Beth down from his mum's arms and gave her a cuddle, before gently lifting her back into her pushchair and fastening her in. After reluctantly saying his farewells to his best friend, he heaved the pushchair back over the rough ground towards the road. Finally, as he closed the five-bar gate and manoeuvred the pushchair wheels back on to the smooth tarmac, a thought entered his head: like Beth, he was hungry. Suddenly, going home for tea and leaving Calum and the fishing behind didn't feel quite so bad after all.

Billy watched, concern written all over his face, as his mum sat back on the blue plastic dining chair and lit a cigarette.

'Mum, do you *have* to do that? We had another PSE session at school today and they kept going on and on about the dangers of smoking.'

'Sorry, Billy . . . It's my nerves.'

'And another thing,' Billy went on, 'it's bad for Beth and me – it affects us too. "Passive smoking" they call it.'

'Sorry, Billy . . . I know you're right – it's just that ever since your dad left . . .'

At the mention of 'Dad', the mood in the kitchen changed. Billy felt concerned for his mum. 'It's OK, Mum. I'll just open a window. Anyway, it's time I got stuck in.'

Beth gurgled from her highchair. She made a noise that sounded remotely like 'stuck in' and Billy and his mum laughed together.

After climbing up on a rickety old kitchen stool and opening the top window, Billy rolled up his sleeves and set to work. Within five minutes he'd cleared the table, got all the dirty pots into a sink full of hot water and was ready to attack the dishes.

He watched his mum lean back in her chair again and close her eyes. He knew that she relied heavily on him whenever she felt 'down'.

Since his dad had walked out just before Beth had been born, Billy had tried to take his place: be the man about the house, help Mum cope with the workload and give her a few minutes off. His mum said he'd not only taken his dad's place, he'd actually done a far better job!

'Cup of tea, Mum?' Billy asked, knowing full-well what the answer would be.

'Oh, Billy, that would be lovely . . . I'm gasping.'

Billy filled the kettle and gazed at his mum's worn-out expression. She took a long drag on her cigarette, opened her eyes and smiled at him. 'What would I do without my Billy-boy?' she said quietly. 'You're a very special boy, Billy. Do you know that?'

Billy looked away, embarrassed, and plugged in the kettle. He reached for the tea caddy and put two heaped spoonfuls of tea into the old brown teapot – his mum still insisted on making tea the old-fashioned way. 'I can't be that special, Mum. We got our assessment results today and I was bottom of the class – as usual!'

'Well, you're not bottom of my class, Billy-boy. You're a top man.'

A few minutes later, the kitchen was clean and everything back in its place. Billy placed two mugs on the draining board, poured a little milk into each, and felt pleased with himself as he poured the tea. If he couldn't come top in exams, he knew he was a dab hand at practical things like cooking meals and keeping the house clean . . . And in any case, what was more useful – being good at maths or being helpful around the house? He knew what his mother would say.

Billy and his mum sipped their tea whilst Beth sat on the floor and tried to build some wooden bricks into a tower. She only ever seemed to manage three and then they fell down with a clatter.

'Mum, do you think I could have a fishing rod for my birthday. I don't mind if it's a second-hand one.'

'I'll have a think about it,' his mum replied. 'I suppose I could put a few more hours in—'

'No, I don't want you to have to work extra or anything like that,' Billy interrupted. 'You'd only have to pay Mrs Ockerby more money to look after Beth – and then it's hardly worth it.'

His mother looked back at him with a furrowed brow. 'Do you know, Billy, there aren't many kids your age that would think like that. As I keep on saying, you're a special boy. Now drink your tea and give the leaves a swirl.'

Billy nodded.

His mum had always claimed to be able to read palms and tealeaves, and some of the neighbours really believed she had 'the gift' – as old Mrs Ockerby called it. But not Billy! He didn't believe in all that mumbo jumbo. The way he looked at it, if Mum had any special powers then why would she be in the mess she was in – no husband, no money and not much of a life to shout about? But all the same, Billy went along with her, just to keep her happy.

He took a final sip of his tea, walked over to the sink, swirled his cup around and emptied the dregs down the plughole.

'Now let's have a look,' his mum said, lifting Beth off the floor and on to her knee.

Billy didn't even bother looking. He'd looked so many times before – and all he ever saw was the usual soggy mess of tealeaves stuck around the bottom and sides of the cup.

He handed her his mug and started walking towards the front room – there was a good programme on the telly that he wanted to see.

But as his mum took the mug and looked into the bottom she went very quiet. This was unusual. The normal routine was for her to start babbling on about how lucky Billy was, and how everything was going to work out fine for him, and how he would almost certainly have a good life and all that. But this time she seemed taken aback and said nothing.

'Are you OK, Mum?' Billy asked.

'Er . . . I'm fine, Billy-boy . . . just fine. I said you were special, but just how much – well, I think I'm only just beginning to realise. Here, take a look.'

She handed the mug back to Billy, but before he had a chance to take it, a gust of wind suddenly whistled in through the kitchen window. Beth pointed up at the light fitting as it rocked from side to side. 'Where did that come from?' his mother asked, as he finally took the cup and looked down into it.

He almost dropped it in surprise.

This time the tealeaves were very different.

They had somehow swirled around the bottom of the cup and arranged themselves into a perfectly-formed letter 'S'.

8
Strange Happenings

'Billy – look closer! Tell me what you've done wrong.'

Billy chewed the end of his pencil and stared at the numbers. He hated numbers. They always seemed to merge into each other. 'Eight add seven . . .'

'Yes.'

'. . . make fifteen.'

'Yes.'

'One down and carry five.'

'No! Think about it!'

Billy studied the numbers more closely. And then he realised his error.

'Oops – should have been five down and carry one, Miss.'

'At last! Well done, Billy. Now put it right.'

Billy stopped chewing the rubber on the end of his pencil and rubbed out the wrong answer. A few minutes later he had the correct answer: eight hundred and sixty-five. 'That looks right now, Miss.'

'Well, I don't know what you mean when you say it *looks* right, Billy. But it is right. And you could get them all right if you just tried to concentrate a bit harder. Anyway, that'll do for now. It's time you were away to your next lesson. The bell's about to go.'

But Billy just kept on staring at the answer: eight-six-five. He didn't know why it looked right either, but there was something about those numbers that seemed significant. As Billy began chewing the end of his pencil again, the bell went, snapping him out of his trance. He packed his books away, left the Learning Support room and headed off to join Calum and the rest of his class in the art block.

He found himself almost sprinting down the corridor. Art was his favourite subject. It was the one subject in which he sometimes performed better than the other pupils. His teacher once said something about him having a real talent for it. Brilliant!

The pupils of 7HC chatted amongst themselves, waiting for Mr Dempster to arrive. The old art teacher was always late. He was disorganised, forever losing things, and he never really knew what he was going to do until five minutes after the lesson had started, but all the kids seemed to like him — especially Billy!

'So how many did you catch?' Billy asked, reaching into his school bag.

'Four more roach and a perch. The perch was a good 'un. It put up a great scrap.'

'Wow . . . Brilliant! What does a perch look like?'

'It has black and yellow stripes and a spiky dorsal fin. Dad says they're predators and hunt in packs.'

Billy's eyes opened even wider than Calum's. He suddenly wanted to catch a perch very badly – Calum made the fish sound so fierce and striking, like a warrior.

'You're lucky to have a dad that goes fishing.'

'I know . . . but as Dad teaches me, I can teach you. And we're both lucky to have a pond to practise in – right by the school.'

Billy nodded thoughtfully as Mr Dempster made his late entry.

'OK, 7DF – sorry I'm late . . .'

Billy and Calum nudged each other and laughed quietly.

Five minutes later, each member of 7HC had a blank A3 sheet of paper in front of them and an array of pencils ranging from very hard to very soft. Mr Dempster explained how the pencils were graded.

'Now, what I want you to do today is this. I want you to pick up a pencil, close your eyes and allow your hand to move freely over the paper in as random a way as possible.'

'What does "random" mean, Sir?' someone towards the back shouted.

'It means that you don't plan where you're going to put your pencil or think too hard about what you're doing. I want you to finish up with a jumble of lines and dots.'

'What good is that, Sir?' a girl near the front asked.

'Francesca, be patient! I'm just coming to that. When you open your eyes and look at the "mess" that you think you've created, I want you to study it very carefully and see if you can see anything within it that stands out — something that you can go over with a darker pencil so that you finish up with a picture or an object worth looking at.'

Lots of pupils began chattering to each other and Billy looked thoughtful. It sounded like a great idea — something different — and it sounded as if it just might work.

A small boy in the middle of the class, who always came top in everything, put up his hand.

'What is it, Charles?'

'Well, Sir — what you've asked us to do is a bit like when you lie on your back and look up at the sky. Sometimes you can see faces in the shapes of the clouds — wild animals and monsters and things. It's the same sort of idea in a way, Sir.'

Some of the pupils began to laugh, but the old art teacher raised his hands and brought silence back to the class.

'Charles is exactly right. Just the same sort of idea. But instead of clouds, you're going to be looking at a series of abstract lines and dots. Now let's give it a go.'

Billy couldn't wait.

He chose a soft pencil — a 2B — closed his eyes, and

allowed the point to hover over the blank paper. Being so poor at maths and things like that, Billy reckoned he would have no problem in producing a random pattern. And so he set to work: his hand moving fast . . . lines and dots – the minutes ticked by – dots and lines. With his eyes still tightly closed, Billy sensed that his hand was moving in a very strange way. And then he stopped.

He looked down and couldn't believe his eyes.

What Billy had actually produced staggered everyone, including Mr Dempster – *but nobody more so than himself!*

Billy found himself running out of the school gates. He was so excited about the rolled-up piece of A3 paper tucked under his arm. For once, he was looking forward to his homework – to finish off the task that the art teacher had set them.

Calum had stayed behind to fish the Forge Pond again and had offered to let Billy have another go. But tonight was Mum's bingo night – the only night she had time to herself whilst Billy looked after Beth for a couple of hours. As much as he yearned to have a second bash at the fishing, there was no way he could bring himself to deny his mum her one night out. In any case, right now, he was more excited about what had happened in the art room.

He trotted on and found himself craning his head back, looking up at the sky. Grey clouds scurried above his head, blowing in the same direction as he was running. Billy thought about what Charlie Hemmingway had said – about trying to see shapes in the clouds. He stopped and stared upwards. Yes . . . it was easy to pick out the outlines of the warriors. Each of the small clouds looked like a curved helmet, the rough bits around their edges looked like tips of spears and swords . . . and a couple of bigger clouds looked like horses . . . and suddenly the whole sky became a battlefield.

'*Are you OK, son?*'

Billy looked in front. It was Mr Haynes, a neighbour. He looked at Billy questioningly.

'Oh, hi, Mr Haynes. Yes ... I'm fine.'

The man gazed upwards. 'What are you staring at? You've not seen a flying saucer, have you?'

'No. I thought I heard a loud plane, that's all,' Billy replied. He was too embarrassed to explain the real reason he'd been gazing up.

Mr Haynes continued to stare skywards, straining to see the plane that Billy knew wasn't there.

'It's gone now,' Billy quickly added. 'I think it disappeared behind a cloud.'

Mr Haynes frowned and walked on. Billy waited until he was well out of sight and then looked up again.

The sky had turned overcast – more clouds had rolled in and formed a grey blanket. The warriors had all gone. Billy imagined that the army had charged on and were waiting for him on his doorstep. It was only fantasy, he knew that – but it thrilled him to think of it.

Still clutching the rolled-up paper under his arm, he sprinted on down the street of terraced houses, ready to meet the soldiers waiting outside his door.

'Slay the enemy!' he shouted to himself.

Just as Billy reached his doorstep, a big drop of water fell on his head. The sky had grown even darker and it started to rain. As he turned the door handle, he took a last look up at the blackening sky. There was one huge black cloud that had crept under the thickening grey blanket. Billy felt compelled to stand there and stare at it as it swirled around his field of vision, constantly changing in shape and size. And then he felt a shock wave run through his body as his brain registered the image before him.

The cloud had formed into an almost perfect picture: a fearsome warrior's helmet with sinister hollowed eye sockets – and it seemed to be glaring straight down at him.

Billy lay tucked under his duvet, thinking about the day's events.

He grabbed the rolled-up paper from his bedside cabinet, stepped into his slippers and crept out on to the landing. He heard his mum snoring quietly and it sounded reassuring. She had come back from bingo in the best mood for ages – and no wonder! She'd won fifty pounds and had promised to think about buying him a fishing rod.

He looked over to Beth's small room. He could just make out the cot and see a dark shape lying quite still in the bottom of it. It seemed his sister was also in a deep sleep.

Brilliant!

He crept on, making his way down the narrow stairs, the sound of the wind outside increasing all the time. It whistled around the house and made the curtains move – as if unseen hands were gently shaking them.

Billy sneaked into the kitchen and groped around in the semi-darkness until he found the drawer by the side of the sink unit. It had all sorts of oddments inside: string, elastic bands, and candles for use in emergency.

Billy took the biggest candle and went to another drawer, where the matches were kept. A few minutes later he had the candle burning brightly at the centre of the kitchen table. He didn't dare put the light on, because he knew that the glass-panelled kitchen door would throw too much light upstairs and disturb his mum – and then she would be sure to come downstairs and investigate.

He sat at the table and carefully unrolled the paper, weighting it down with the butter dish on one end and a heavy ashtray on the other. He pulled the candle closer and lit up the strange image he'd somehow drawn that very afternoon.

It was a collection of very dark curvy lines sprouting from the outline of a semi-circle. The lines were so tightly compacted that someone had said they looked like hair. Mr Dempster had said that he couldn't believe it to be a random pattern and that something in Billy's mind must have been guiding him when he drew it. And this thought had greatly intrigued Billy — and this was the reason why he was here now: he just couldn't resist carrying on, to see how it all came out.

He picked up the 2B pencil. How should he continue? It was difficult to know how to finish something that he didn't recognise in the first place . . . Maybe he should just close his eyes again.

Billy pushed the candle away and allowed the darkness to envelop the drawing. And then he closed his eyes and stretched his hand out over the paper. He gasped and swallowed hard as the pencil went to work. Again, his hand seemed to move of its own accord — working on one area of the paper and then moving to another. It felt as if he was being guided, and he began to feel afraid.

As Billy worked on, the candle burnt lower and his shadow grew sharper in front of him. His silhouette seemed unreal — statue-like . . . only the drawing hand moving up and down . . . the pencil making a ghostly rasping sound as it continued its work.

As the scribbling progressed, Billy opened his eyes and watched the semi-circle turn into an oval, and then the whole thing began to look more and more like some sort of helmet. The wavy lines that someone had said looked like hair now looked even more like hair, sprouting out from the edges of the helmet.

Billy couldn't understand it. It was beginning to look like the image he'd seen in the clouds glaring down at him!

His hand worked on — putting more and more detail into the drawing. And all the time, the weather outside grew wilder. The wind whistled ever louder, moaning down the chimney and causing the windowpanes to rattle as if something outside was trying to get in.

Billy hoped his mum wouldn't wake and come downstairs.

Meanwhile, two hundred miles away, a giant shadow, full of wrath and anger, stalked a lonely fen . . . waiting for the 'special' boy, determined to smash his young bones to pulp . . . knowing that the time was finally drawing near.

9
Holidays

'Billy! Are you OK? You look tired.'

If only Mum knew, Billy thought to himself. He'd been up most of the night, trying to finish off the mysterious picture. He looked across at the rolled-up paper, tied with an elastic band, sitting on top of the fridge. He still couldn't believe it – his mind reeled at the thought of it.

'Billy! Are you listening to me? What's wrong? You haven't heard a word I've said.'

'Sorry, Mum. I was just thinking about something.'

He poured a little cooking oil into the hot frying pan and waited for it to bubble. The raw bacon was on a plate by his side and Billy had already trimmed the fat off with a pair of scissors.

'You seem to be doing a lot of thinking these days, Billy-boy. You're growing up fast – maybe a bit too fast. Anyway, I've got something to say.'

Billy placed three rashers of bacon in the hot pan and watched it sizzle. He pushed it around with a fork and turned the gas down as a splash of hot fat sprayed on to his hand. Beth gurgled in her highchair and banged her plastic mug on the tray.

'Quiet, Beth! Let Billy concentrate,' Billy's mum said firmly.

For the next few minutes, nobody spoke as Billy focused on the frying pan and produced two doorstep bacon butties.

'Now, as I was saying, Billy, I've got some news – good news!'

Billy watched his mum take a bite of her sandwich and smile across at him. 'Go on then, Mum. Tell me!'

His mum smiled again, taking her time, teasing him. 'Well . . . when you break up for half-term, me and Beth are going to stay with your Auntie Emily.'

Billy tried desperately to work out where all this was leading. 'And what about me?'

'Well, that's the good news. Calum's mum rang me last night, after you'd gone to bed. They want to take you with them on a week's holiday. Well, almost a week. They're going on the Sunday and coming back on Friday night. It's got to fit in with Mr Truelove's work.'

Billy felt a shiver of excitement. He'd never been on a proper holiday. The nearest he'd got to it was a week with Auntie Emily. She lived in a run-down seaside resort on the east coast, and had taken Billy and his family on the beach a couple of times.

'Where are they going? Calum's never mentioned it.'

'That's because Calum doesn't know yet. He's only finding out this morning. They're going to Norfolk, to a little village close to the sea – and there's lots of fishing. Mr Truelove says that he and Calum have got enough spare fishing gear for you to use, and – if you really enjoy it – then I'll use some of my bingo winnings to buy you your own rod for your birthday. How about that, Billy?'

Billy stopped chewing. His mum laughed at his shocked expression. He really couldn't get his head around it: a holiday with his best friend . . . a fishing holiday . . . in a real holiday place . . . for a week.

He took another bite of his bacon buttie and beamed a radiant smile back across the table. Brilliant! And then a sudden thought entered his mind.

'Becky! Will she be going?'

Billy's mum smiled again. 'Of course she will. I think she's taking a friend too.'

Two thirteen-year-old girls, Billy thought glumly. *Calum's sister and her best friend, Samantha Redgate – both of them an absolute pain!*

'And Dad says we can go fishing just about every day,' Calum said excitedly. 'There's the River Yare close by and some dykes. One of the dykes is only about two minutes from the windmill.'

'Windmill?' Billy gasped. 'What do you mean, "windmill"?'

Calum laughed and rocked back on his chair. 'We're staying in a converted windmill. I'll show you the brochure when you're round at our house again. It looks fantastic. There's about five floors and if I get my way we'll be sleeping right at the top.'

'Sounds brilliant!' Billy exclaimed. 'And will we have it to ourselves?'

Calum knew exactly where Billy was coming from. 'Yes . . . well away from Becky and Sam – they're on the floor below. And Mum and Dad on the floor below them.'

'So Samantha Redgate's going?'

'Yeah – I know she's a pain, but then so is Becky. They'll be good company for each other and they're bound to keep out of our way for most of the time. They'll be off shopping with Mum or sunning themselves on the beach or doing all that other girly stuff. And we'll be off exploring and fishing and having a great time. I can't wait!'

Billy's heart leapt at the thought of it. It would be the greatest adventure ever!

He'd just decided to ask Calum more details about the fishing when Mrs Calthrop arrived. She sat at her desk, filled in the register and signalled Billy to walk over.

'Lesson one: history with Mr Wild – he's got a visitor and

he wants you in on it, Billy. He thinks you'll really enjoy it.'

'So I don't need to go to Learning Support, Miss?'

'No – I've already had a word with Mrs Webb. She's fine about it and she's going to look in on you from time to time, to check that you're coping with everything.'

'Brilliant, Miss!'

Mrs Calthrop smiled as Billy scurried back to his seat.

'Today we have a visitor,' Mr Wild said, full of enthusiasm.

Along with the other pupils, Billy stared at the stranger by Mr Wild's side.

'He looks old,' Calum whispered.

Billy looked at the man's white hair, bushy white eyebrows and matching beard, and nodded in agreement.

'I want you to start a new page and put today's date. We're about to start an interesting little project,' Mr Wild said enthusiastically.

Billy leant over his learning support book and concentrated hard on writing the date neatly in the top right-hand corner of the page. He didn't want to appear different to the others in the class and took his time, desperately trying to keep the writing exactly on the lines. That done, he looked up and saw Mr Wild rubbing his hands together and looking straight at him.

'Billy Hardacre . . .'

Billy cringed. He hated questions. The last thing he wanted was to make a fool of himself in front of everyone.

'Yes, Sir?'

'Billy, don't worry – I'm not going to put you on the spot. I was just going to say that I'm glad you're with us today because our visitor, Dr Smedley, is a leading authority on a subject that fascinates everyone.'

Billy felt himself relax a little.

'And the reason for that,' Mr Wild continued, rubbing his hands even harder together, 'is because it involves some of the most ruthless, savage invaders that the world has ever known.'

Everyone in 7HC suddenly sat up.

Mr Wild turned his gaze away from Billy and faced the rest of the class. 'And does anyone know where these fearsome invaders came from?' he asked the sea of expectant faces. 'Try to think back to when you were at your primary school – probably in Year 4.'

'*Scandinavia, Sir – from Norway, Denmark and Sweden.*'

Everyone swivelled on their seat to see who had answered the question so quickly and confidently. Mr Wild and Dr Smedley looked more than impressed. Calum almost fell off his chair – it was the boy by his side!

Billy!

'Wow! That Viking stuff must have made quite an impression on you, Billy,' Calum whispered, his eyes wide with surprise. 'I can't remember much about it . . . except that the Vikings were cool warriors.'

Billy nodded, looked down at his book and said nothing.

* * *

That night, Billy lay in bed going over and over the day's events.

He had surprised everybody in the history lesson, none more so than himself. How could he possibly have known the answer to Mr Wild's question? He'd never seen or heard of anything to do with Viking raiders before – he'd been away ill in Year 4 and had missed the entire topic.

Calum had said that Billy must have read about it somewhere – how else could he have known? The rest of the class, especially Charlie Hemmingway, had been gobsmacked. It was the first time anyone could remember Billy Hardacre answering a question at all – never mind one so quickly.

The rest of the lesson had enthralled everyone – the Vikings were so powerful, so scary. And Billy had listened to Dr Smedley like he'd never listened to anyone before. The visitor seemed to know everything about them, and Billy had hung on every word. At lunchtime he'd gone straight to the school library and taken out a book all about the Vikings and now it lay on his bedside cabinet by the side of the rolled-up paper.

A confusion of thoughts began to swirl around in his mind.

He thought back to the perfectly formed letter 'S' in the bottom of his mug. Was it really a sign that he was special? Did his mum really have some sort of power? If *she* did, then why shouldn't *he*? After all, he *was* her son.

He thought about the maths lesson in Learning Support – how the numbers 'eight-six-five' had stood out and seemed special. In fact, lots of 'special' things seemed to be happening at the moment – the thrill of catching his first fish, the weird cloud formations . . . Or was it all just in his imagination?

Billy tried to calm his mind and get some sleep. But just as he began to doze, slipping into gentle slumber, a sharp rapping on his bedroom window jolted him back to wakefulness.

Jumping out of bed, he drew back the curtains – *and recoiled in horror!*

A huge black bird stared in at him with evil beady eyes.

Billy shrieked . . . but the bird screeched even louder as it took off into the crisp night air and disappeared over the chimney tops.

10
Familiar Surroundings

Mr and Mrs Truelove spoke quietly in the front seat of the people-carrier.

Becky and her friend, Samantha Redgate, chatted loudly behind them, and Calum talked on and on about fishing to Billy in the back.

But Billy heard little of Calum's conversation.

Soothed by the gentle roar of the car engine, he struggled to keep his eyes open. He slipped into a doze. He hadn't slept well for ages, what with the bird incident and everything else that had been happening, and now the excitement of the holiday having finally arrived . . .

'Billy! You're not listening!' Calum suddenly exclaimed.

Becky turned round and glared, 'I don't blame him!' she muttered, looking back to Sam and smiling. 'You only ever talk a load of rubbish!'

'Get stuffed!' Calum retorted.

The two girls giggled and looked away.

'That's enough, you two!' Mrs Truelove turned round and intervened. 'Don't spoil things – you've been good up to now!'

'OK, folks . . .' Mr Truelove shouted over his shoulder. 'We're turning off the A1 – at the next services we'll pull up for a loo stop and a snack. Is everyone in agreement?'

Calum, Becky and Samantha Redgate all shouted their approval. Billy's eyes flickered open and he smiled and nodded his head.

'That's it then!' Mr Truelove said. 'I think the decision's unanimous.'

Billy didn't know what the word 'unanimous' meant, but as the people-carrier turned on to the A17, heading towards Sleaford, he suddenly got the creepiest feeling that they were being followed. He looked over his shoulder and through the rear window – just a van behind, the young driver busy chatting to a girl by his side. Perhaps it was just his imagination. Who could possibly want to follow them? But if Billy had been able to see up through the roof above his head, he might just have been able to make out a large black bird – *gliding directly above them and tracking their every move!*

As the people-carrier travelled down the A47 during the final stage of their journey, Billy stared quietly out of the window.

The landscape was so different – vast and flat. The skyline was dotted with numerous windmills in various states of repair – some complete with sails, some without. Herds of cattle grazed the sparsely-vegetated pastures, the flat fields separated by small embankments and dykes instead of hedgerows and fences.

The scene should have been completely alien to Billy – he had never been anywhere like this before – and yet, in some strange way, it all seemed familiar.

It was so confusing!

'I think we're almost there,' Mrs Truelove said, consulting the map. 'Take the next right, darling . . . We should reach Fenthorpe after another half a mile.'

Billy smiled to himself. He knew that Mrs Truelove always called her husband 'darling' when she was in a good mood.

'And then when we reach the church we turn right and head off deeper into the marshes, don't we?'

'Yes, darling. Here's the church now . . . and there's the right turn.'

Everyone in the car went quiet and stared out of the window.

'Now, according to our instructions, we swing left by Fenthorpe Grange and then look for another left turn a bit further on . . .'

Calum gasped and peered out of the window as a large, Gothic-style house appeared on the left-hand side of the road. 'Wow, that looks like the creepiest house I've ever seen,' he commented as the car slowed. He tugged on Billy's sleeve.

'Small boy, big imagination,' Becky quipped back at him. 'It's just an old house – that's all!'

As the car turned and cruised past the mansion, Billy gawped at the giant stone pillars capped with stone eagles standing at the end of the short gravelled driveway. He tried to see more, but the car picked up speed and they were past – no time to take in anything else.

'Now where's this next left turn?' Mr Truelove asked, beginning to slow down again.

'It can't be far . . . It's called Plunderers' Lane,' Mrs Truelove replied, straining to see ahead.

'Great name!' Mr Truelove smiled. 'But I can't see any turnings.'

It was Billy who spoke up. 'There – just by that dead tree.'

Silence fell in the car as Mr Truelove slowed and turned. Billy was right – a sign half-hidden by bushes read 'PLUNDERERS' LANE'.

'Hey . . . how did you know that?' Calum asked, his voice full of surprise.

Billy didn't answer – he was just as surprised as Calum.

As Mr Truelove drove slowly forward, everyone stared in anticipation through the front windscreen. After another minute, a group of farm buildings appeared in front of them; a rough track curved off to the left.

Calum's dad turned down the track, and a few seconds later they all cheered as the windmill appeared in the distance.

Billy leant over and whispered to Calum: 'I know it sounds weird, but I feel as if I've been here before.'

Samantha overheard him. She turned around and stared. 'You're beginning to sound spooky.'

'Boys are spooky, full stop!' Becky chipped in, a bored look spreading across her face.

'Well...' Mr Truelove said, as he stopped the car outside the windmill and pulled on the handbrake. 'We're here.'

Mrs Truelove nodded and smiled, folding the map away at the same time.

Calum dived out of the door. 'First in gets first choice of bedrooms . . . Quick, Billy – let's get in there!'

'NO! MUM! IT'S NOT FAIR!' Becky yelled, diving out of the car and trying to catch up with him.

'Leave them to it, Billy,' Mr Truelove frowned. 'I promised your mother you'd phone her as soon as we got here. Here – use my mobile and let her know we've arrived safely.'

Billy thanked Mr Truelove and took the phone. He climbed slowly out of the car and scanned around, taking in the landscape – vast flat marshes stretching as far as the eye could see. There was a distinct smell of damp vegetation in the air and somewhere in the distance an animal's cry rang out across the marsh.

It all seemed so natural . . . so familiar.

Billy shivered a little.

He wasn't cold. It was a strange feeling that suddenly came over him – a definite feeling of unease . . .

11
Home from Home

'Hi, Mum. Yes, I can hear you.'

Billy paced around outside the windmill holding Mr Truelove's mobile close to his ear. As he spoke, he looked up at the window under the white domed roof and saw Calum waving down at him. Calum had got the room right at the top. Brilliant!

'Now, Billy! Listen to me! I want you to keep in touch. Phone me every now and then, just so that I know you're OK – and everything *is* OK, isn't it?'

Billy wondered whether or not to tell her about the strange goings-on. 'Brilliant, Mum! It's great here . . . You should see the windmill.'

There was a pause before she spoke again. 'Do as Mr and Mrs Truelove tell you, won't you, Billy-boy? Don't go doing anything stupid. Watch out for yourself.'

This last instruction made him feel uneasy again.

He looked nervously over his shoulder and took a deep breath before he spoke. 'Don't worry, Mum – I'll be fine.'

Calum banged on the window, gesturing for him to finish his conversation and come on up. It gave Billy the excuse he needed. 'I've got to go now, Mum. I'll phone again tomorrow. Try not to worry.'

'OK, Billy – take care. Beth and Aunt Emily send their love.'

Billy switched off the mobile and walked towards the windmill; it cast a huge pepper-pot shadow under the setting sun. Feeling jittery, he trotted the last few yards and pushed open the door of this unusual sanctuary – home for himself and the Truelove family for the next six days.

Billy finished unpacking and sat on the top bunk. Calum had given Billy first choice of beds and so Billy had chosen the top.

'This is brilliant!' he kept on saying.

Calum was busy transferring some socks and pants from his travel bag into the bottom drawer of an old wooden dresser on the opposite side of the room. Billy stared out of the window and called over to him. 'I can see for miles.'

'I know . . . It's great up here,' Calum replied. 'It's like having our own top-floor flat.'

Billy nodded and looked around the strange room. It was small, with eight walls made of wood (octagonal-shaped,

Mrs Truelove had said) – the walls tapering up to a wooden ceiling. A small panel stood out in the centre of the ceiling; Mr Truelove said it probably led to some sort of loft space at the very top of the windmill.

Over by the dresser, a big trapdoor opened on to a ladder that led down to the floor below. This was Becky and Sam's bedroom. For safety reasons, the trapdoor had to be kept closed – to stop Billy or Calum from accidentally falling through it. And in any case, the girls had quickly pointed out that they did not want two silly boys peering down at them from above. In fact, they'd insisted on the boys knocking on the trapdoor before opening it, just in case they were getting changed or something.

'And you'd better not make a lot of noise, banging and crashing about over our heads,' Becky had warned.

'Don't worry, wouldn't want to ruin your beauty sleep – you need it!' Calum had quipped back, making Billy laugh out loud. And then Sam had scowled at him – making him giggle even more.

'The windmill's brilliant,' Billy said, looking back through the window again. 'I love the wooden stairs everywhere.'

'Me too,' Calum nodded, stuffing the last pair of socks into the dresser. 'The stairs are cool! Did you hear Mum moaning? She said she'll probably get fed up of them – there's no pleasing some people!'

At the mention of Calum's mum, Billy suddenly went quiet.

'Are you OK?' Calum asked.

'Just thinking about Mum,' Billy replied, looking out of the window again.

Calum climbed the ladder on to the top bunk and sat beside him. 'No need to worry about her,' he smiled. 'She's tough, your mum.'

'Calum, if I tell you something, will you promise not to tell anyone?'

'Course – I can keep a secret. What's up?'

Billy turned to face his friend and looked him straight in the eye. 'I've been feeling really weird lately. I've got a nervous feeling in my stomach.'

Calum sat cross-legged by his side. 'That bird tapping on your bedroom window would freak anyone out.'

'And the strange goings-on at school . . .' Billy added.

'What do you mean?'

'The drawing I did in the art lesson – that was really weird. And the question I answered in the history lesson – about the Vikings. I didn't know anything about Vikings.'

Calum nodded thoughtfully.

'And then – this business of feeling I've been here before,' Billy stammered.

Both boys sat staring at one another, neither sure what to say next, when the trapdoor opened over by the dresser. 'Come on, you two – supper's on the table. We're all waiting.'

Billy and Calum looked across at Mr Truelove's head

sticking up through the floor. His glasses were perched precariously on the end of his nose.

'OK, Dad,' Calum replied.

'Come on then – get a move on!' he said, as his head disappeared back down below.

Calum and Billy followed – Billy at the back. Just as Billy took another step down the ladder, so that only his head stuck up above the trapdoor, he heard a loud crash that seemed to come from the bedroom ceiling.

'Did you hear that?' he shouted downwards.

But Calum was hungry and had already moved down through the girls' room and was descending the next flight of steps.

Billy quickly climbed down and caught up. He felt a sudden nervousness as he realised that the bang had come from the loft space – *above his bed!*

That night, Billy lay in the top bunk desperately trying to get to sleep, Calum snoring gently beneath him. There were no noises from the loft space – he'd mentioned it during supper and Mr Truelove had reassured him that it would probably be due to mice or birds. But Billy knew that it would have taken more than a small animal to make the loud bang he'd heard earlier.

He lay back with his hands behind his head, going over everything that had happened, and became more and more restless. The room was shrouded in darkness and, judging by the silence that had enveloped the entire windmill, Billy guessed that everyone down below must be asleep.

Finally, beginning to relax a little, he snuggled under the duvet and yawned in readiness for welcome sleep — *and that's when he heard the footsteps coming up the wooden steps from the girls' room below.*

12
Making Plans

'Billy, I really am so sorry . . . I didn't mean to scare you last night.'

Becky and Sam giggled, and even Calum joined in – nudging Billy and making a scary face at the same time.

'It's OK, Mrs Truelove.'

'I'll do the final check-around tonight,' Mr Truelove said, as he sliced a white loaf on the worktop, 'and I'll knock three times on the trapdoor first so you know it's me. We don't want to frighten anyone again.'

'But we might be asleep, Dad. And then you'll wake us.'

Mr Truelove walked over to the large circular table in the centre of the room and placed a plate of toast close to Billy's plate of bacon and eggs. 'I'll just have to knock gently then.'

'In any case, who did you think it was, Billy? The Phantom of the Windmill?' Becky teased.

Billy said nothing. He forced a smile and carried on eating.

'Leave him alone!' Calum snapped, suddenly thinking about the conversation he'd had with Billy the night before. 'Just remember that if this place is haunted, the ghost will get to your room before ours.'

'Unless it lives up in the loft,' Samantha chipped in.

'*Whooo-hhh*,' Becky added in ghostly fashion, sneering back at her brother.

Mrs Truelove brought over another plate of bacon and eggs from the stove and placed it in front of her husband. 'OK, that's enough. We need to get on. We've got a busy day ahead of us.'

'What are the plans, Dad?' Becky asked.

'Well, we thought we could all go into Yarmouth this morning and do some shopping, and this afternoon I might take the boys fishing while you girls go on the beach.'

'Wicked, Dad!' Calum spluttered as he chewed on a mouthful of breakfast. 'Me and Billy would love to go fishing . . . and the weather looks good – I poked my head out earlier.'

'Sounds good to me, too,' Becky joined in. 'We can get those beach sandals we talked about, Sam, and you could look for that new bikini.'

Sam spread some butter on a piece of toast and nodded enthusiastically.

'OK! That's decided then!' Mr Truelove said. 'I'll drive back and pick you girls up from the beach around five o'clock – the boys can fish on until we get back.'

'Will they be OK on their own?' Mrs Truelove asked, staring across at Billy.

'I thought we'd fish a dyke close to here – literally five minutes away. I'm sure they can fish safely on their own, and if they get fed up they can pack up and come back here. I'll leave a spare key hidden outside the door.'

Billy nodded his approval and tucked into his breakfast. He felt the excitement well up inside. Like Calum, he couldn't wait to sample the fishing.

Within the hour, the table had been cleared, the breakfast pots washed and put away (Becky and Sam had reluctantly taken first turn on the washing up rota) and everyone was seated in the people-carrier.

As Mr Truelove reversed the car and manoeuvred it back on to the rough track, no one saw the black beady eyes staring down, watching their every move from a hole in the white domed roof at the top of the windmill.

Billy and Calum looked in wonder at the array of brightly-coloured fishing floats lining the counter.

'A pint of maggots in each of these, please,' Mr Truelove requested, handing two plastic bait containers to a man who looked quite old, with thick white hair and a matching moustache. He took the containers and disappeared through a door into the back of the shop.

'Wow! Look at that!' Calum suddenly shouted, pointing up at the wall.

Billy's eyes bulged in disbelief at the size of the pike in its long glass case. 'There's some writing scratched on the glass,' he pointed out to Calum, 'but I can't make it out.'

Mr Truelove stepped up to the counter, leant across and read out the inscription:

Caught by Tom Walters
15th February 1947
River Yare — Cantley
32lbs 8ozs

'That is some pike,' Mr Truelove added, just as the man returned with their bait.

'Anything else, Sir?'

'Yes. We're staying in a converted windmill up at Fenthorpe. Do we need any special licences to fish the dykes?'

As Mr Truelove spoke, Billy watched the pained expression spread across the old shopkeeper's face. 'You don't want to bother with the dykes. Try the main river – or better still, get out on to the Broads like everyone else. The dykes are difficult to fish – too complicated.'

Mr Truelove sounded more than surprised at this response. 'What do you mean by "complicated"? I had a quick look at the dyke up by the windmill and it looked good. The banks were fairly flat and there were lots of fish dimpling on the surface.'

The old man coughed, cleared his throat, and looked Mr Truelove straight in the face. 'That'll be Demon's Dyke you're speaking of. You're right – it's full of fish. They swim up from the main river – there's more cover and less current. But let me tell you that dyke is bad news. It's got bad history. Stay away, is my advice!'

Billy looked from the man's serious expression to Calum. And then the two of them looked at Mr Truelove. He smiled back, as if trying to reassure them.

'If you're set on it, you can get day tickets at the Bickerdyke Inn,' the old man continued. 'Dan Turner is the landlord – he owns most of the land and the fishing rights.'

Mr Truelove looked towards the pike in the glass case again. 'You wouldn't happen to be Tom Walters?'

'One and the same, Sir – caught it on the main river, close to where you're staying. And that's where you and the boys should fish – the main river.'

As they drove back towards the windmill, Billy, Calum and Mr Truelove chatted on excitedly about the fishing. They talked about the old man in the shop, the size of the pike in the glass case, but most of all about the old man's reluctance for them to fish Demon's Dyke.

'Do you think the dyke really is dangerous, Dad?' Calum

asked from the back seat (it was Billy's turn to travel in the front). 'Should we keep to the main river, like the man said?'

'We'll have a word with the pub landlord,' Mr Truelove replied. 'If he says it's dangerous, then we'd better do as they say. But it looked safe enough to me when I had a scout round.'

Calum nodded. He was keen to fish the dyke. But as they turned into the car park at the Bickerdyke Inn, Billy found himself beginning to feel distinctly uncomfortable. The mention of the name 'Demon's Dyke' had unsettled him.

Several hours later, three lone fishermen sat along the banks of Demon's Dyke, thoroughly enjoying themselves.

Mr Truelove hadn't caught much — he'd been too busy helping Calum and Billy. But with his assistance, both boys had managed to catch a fair number of small roach. Each one had been in pristine condition and their silvery bodies had glistened in the afternoon sunshine.

As Mr Truelove helped Calum to untangle a knot in his fishing line, Billy sat snugly in his gap in the tall reeds and took in the scene.

The sky overhead was deep blue with a scattering of slow-moving white fluffy clouds. A few birds soared high above and a distant plane made a smoke trail.

At ground level, everything appeared green and lush. The tall reeds on both banks swayed gently in the warm breeze.

They rustled, and Billy imagined that they were whispering to each other, telling tales – maybe the same ones that the pub landlord had spoken of earlier.

Billy allowed his thoughts to drift back to what Dan Turner had said about the stories of weird happenings on the marshes: strange noises and ghostly lights along the dykes, and – most scary of all – the *Fen Phantom!*

The landlord had laughed as he'd told them about the superstition. He'd made it clear that in his opinion it was all a load of old rubbish. 'The fishing's excellent,' the landlord had finally said, as he'd sold them three fishing permits. 'It's good because nobody ever bothers to fish there. They always goes up the main river or the Broads, along with all the other tourists.'

Billy snapped himself back to the present and glanced up and down the undisturbed banks. No sign of any other anglers having been around. No flattened reed stems. No discarded litter.

The landlord was right – nobody did come here.

Billy's float suddenly stopped moving on its gentle course down the centre of the dyke. It wobbled a little and then disappeared below the surface. He jerked his wrist and lifted the rod, just like Calum had taught him. Sure enough, the top section of the thin fibreglass rod arched over.

'I've got one – and it's big!' Billy shrieked.

As Calum and his dad appeared by his side, Billy kept his cool and played the fish gently. He could feel every move the fish made as it dived determinedly towards the bottom of the dyke, deep down and still out of sight.

'Wow! That's a big 'un!' Calum shouted.

'Keep the rod-tip up . . . Wind the reel slowly . . .' Mr Truelove calmly instructed.

A few minutes later, a huge golden slab rolled on the surface. Billy and Calum's eyes almost popped out of their sockets.

'It's a bream, Billy,' Mr Truelove stated. 'And it's got to be at least five pounds in weight.'

Calum reached out with the landing net and a few seconds later, much to everyone's relief, the fish was on the bank by Billy's side.

Mr Truelove helped remove the tiny hook from the fish's leathery lips before the three anglers gazed in admiration at Billy's catch.

Billy thought it was the most wonderful and fascinating creature he'd ever seen. As the bream flapped on the bank amongst the broken reed-stems, Mr Truelove suggested it be returned straight to the water before it suffered any more harm.

With both hands, Billy lowered the fish gently into the dyke and watched with satisfaction as it quickly recovered and swam slowly away into the murky depths.

'Brilliant! I can't believe I caught it,' Billy said, as he wiped the slime from his hands with an old piece of towel.

Mr Truelove and Calum looked touched.

'You aint seen nothing yet, Billy,' Mr Truelove quipped. 'Just wait till a little later. The landlord said there's tench in here. Now they're what you call *real* monsters.'

Calum began explaining to Billy about tench, while Mr Truelove readied himself to go off and collect the girls.

'Now will you two be OK? I should only be about an hour. If you get tired and want to pack up, you know where the spare key is hidden.'

'Somehow I don't think we're going to get fed up, Dad,' Calum said without taking his eyes off the tip of his little float.

'OK . . . but be sensible!'

'We will, Mr Truelove,' Billy shouted from a few metres further downstream.

One and a half hours later, Mr Truelove had not returned. The fishing was still good, and Billy and Calum continued to catch lots of roach and the occasional perch. They chatted on and waited expectantly for the tench to move in. They didn't notice the time, or the fact that Calum's dad was late. They didn't even notice the thick mist descending like a woolly blanket over the entire area.

And they were completely unaware of the strange spectral light that had suddenly materialised from the innermost marshes – moving closer to them with every passing second.

13
Night Stalker

Without warning, the fishing suddenly 'died'.

'Are you still getting bites, Billy?'

Billy couldn't see Calum, hidden further up the bank amongst the reeds, but he could hear him clearly. 'No! Are you?' he shouted back.

'No – it's gone as dead as a doornail. So much for Dad's theory about the tench moving in!'

'What time is it?' Billy asked.

Calum looked at his watch. 'It's half-past seven. I can't remember what time Dad left – it must have been ages ago.'

'I think we'd better pack up,' Billy replied, suddenly feeling a nervous flutter in his stomach. 'Something might have happened.'

Just as Billy began reeling in his line, he became aware of the thick layer of mist lying on top of the reeds on the far bank. And then he looked over his shoulder and saw that the mist was lying across the fields behind. In fact, the only place the mist wasn't lying was on the water in front.

Calum stepped through the reeds by Billy's side. He looked worried. 'Have you seen the mist?'

'Yes – I've just noticed. It's scary!'

As the two boys looked over to the far bank, now completely shrouded, the reeds suddenly erupted and a loud cry filled their ears.

Billy and Calum almost collapsed into the water as a pair of coots scooted away up the far bank in a state of panic.

'God! That frightened the life out of me.'

'Me too,' Billy answered, beginning to pack up his tackle. 'I wonder what scared them?'

Before Calum had chance to reply, Billy crouched down and gestured him to do the same. The silence that suddenly enveloped the dyke was overwhelming. Billy could almost hear his own heartbeat. But there was something else. 'Listen,' Billy whispered softly. 'Can you hear anything?'

'Yes!' Calum whispered back. 'It's like reeds or straw – something rustling . . . It sounds like it's coming from somewhere up the far bank.'

They both stared in the direction of the sound – and saw the distant shimmering light.

'Oh my God! What's that, Billy?'

'I don't know. It can't be your dad, can it?'

'No!' Calum said. 'He wouldn't be on the far bank. And in

any case, that's no torchlight – it looks weird. I don't like it! We'd better pack up – and quick!'

'No time,' Billy said, still staring at the approaching light. 'Just keep down, and keep quiet. Get ready to run.'

As they crouched low, the sound of crushing reed-stems grew louder. The glow from the light grew bigger.

'It's coming straight towards us,' Calum whispered, his voice shaking. 'It's on the far side of the dyke. Let's run while we've got chance.'

'Not yet,' Billy answered quietly. 'We'll get lost in the mist.'

Billy tried to sound calm, but inside, he knew that the thing approaching on the other bank was sinister. His senses were telling him that danger was closing in. Truthfully, at this moment, Billy was more terrified than Calum would ever know.

The tall reeds on the far bank began to move. The light turned into a dull, eerie glow.

Suddenly, the disturbance was directly opposite.

Billy and Calum shuffled up against each other, crouching amongst the near-bank reeds and staring tight-lipped across the dyke. The glow seemed to sit on top of the reeds, illuminating the swirling mist with spectacular effect. Otherwise, there was still nothing to see – until the reeds slowly parted . . .

Billy and Calum gasped as an enormous, warrior-like figure stepped out of the reed cover.

Completely bathed in a yellowish-blue glow and towering taller than any man they'd ever seen, he stood there – motionless, threatening – staring across in their direction. The huge figure shimmered like a phantom and yet it looked solid and real, the reed-stems breaking and cracking beneath its heavy feet.

The two boys crouched – unable to move, in a complete state of shock – each trying to come to terms with the awful vision, their brains desperately trying to make sense of it.

'Can he see us?' Calum finally whispered.

Billy stared across. It was hard to tell because the warrior's head was hidden under the most fearsome helmet he'd ever seen – and yet it looked familiar.

'What's that he's carrying?' Calum whispered again.

In one hand the figure wielded a mighty sword, and in the other – something that neither Calum nor Billy could make out . . . It looked ridiculously like a string shopping bag.

Before Billy had chance to offer a guess, a huge bird suddenly descended from the mist, perched on the warrior's shoulder and let out a piercing shriek that rang out into the damp air. Much to Billy and Calum's horror this seemed to trigger a reaction, as the warrior stepped forward into the water and started wading towards them.

'OH MY GOD! HE'S SEEN US! RUN, BILLY!' Calum screamed.

But Billy needed no telling – he'd already set off, making straight into the swirling mist behind.

'Grab my arm, Calum!' Billy yelled to his friend. 'We need to keep together!'

Stricken with terror, the two boys ran into the mist-shrouded field, clinging to each other and racing onwards, the glow still visible behind.

'It's still there – right behind us!' Calum screamed.

Billy pulled on his friend's arm and ran even faster.

'The windmill must be near,' Billy shouted, desperate to offer some form of encouragement.

And then, without warning, the ground turned swampy beneath their feet.

'WE'RE SINKING!' Calum screamed.

Billy fell over and landed in squelching mud. Calum tried to drag him to his feet and then shrieked out again: 'The light – it's moved. It's right in front of us!'

Billy lay on his stomach in an inch of water, peering into the mist ahead of them. Calum crouched over him. Sure enough, the light was approaching from the opposite direction – straight towards them.

'It's no good!' Calum groaned. 'There's nowhere to go. We're done for!'

Billy knew that Calum was right.

They were sinking into the marsh – and completely stuck.

14
The Fen Phantom

As the tall figure stepped out of the mist, Calum and Billy almost screamed with relief.

'What on earth's going on?' Mr Truelove yelled at them. He stood over the two boys and shone the big battery-powered torch into their muddied, traumatised faces.

'Where have you been, Dad?' Calum yelled back at him, his voice quivering with emotion. 'You said you'd only be an hour!'

'I know . . . I'm sorry – we got a flat tyre. It took ages to get to the tools. I had to take everything out of the boot – and then one of the wheel nuts was seized on. In the end I had to phone the RAC to come out and help. But never mind about me – what on earth's happened to you two?'

Billy dragged himself to his feet as Calum stammered on about the strange sighting. Mr Truelove listened and said nothing. He shone the torch all around in a complete circle, the strong beam penetrating the mist – there was nothing to see.

He led them back to the windmill – which was only minutes away!

As they walked through the door, Mrs Truelove rushed to greet them.

'Thank God!' she cried out. She gasped at the sight of the two boys splattered in mud and wet through to the skin. 'Don't even bother to tell me what happened. The main thing is you're safe! Go and get those wet things off and clean yourselves up while I put the kettle on. You can tell us everything over a hot drink . . . Now get a move on!'

'Disgusting!' Becky said, turning to Sam and making a face.

'Leave them alone, Becky,' Mr Truelove said. 'They've been through enough.'

Neither Billy nor Calum could argue with that, so, without another word, they rushed off towards the bathroom.

Billy thought that the sitting room was the cosiest room in the windmill.

It was on the first floor above the kitchen. A wood-burning stove stood against one of the walls and most of the furniture was arranged in a half-circle around it. Calum and Billy sat on a thick pile rug in front of the stove whilst Becky and Sam sat on the leather sofa. Mr and Mrs Truelove sat in armchairs on either side of them, and everyone sipped hot drinks. A TV stood over to one side of the stove, but tonight it remained off.

Billy stared at the dancing flames through the little glass door of the stove as Calum related what had happened. Billy kept nodding in agreement and throwing in a little more detail from time to time.

Calum's parents and the girls cast curious glances at each other as the boys told their story. When Calum finally described the phantom warrior, Becky and Sam had a fit of the giggles.

'Dad! Tell them! They're just being stupid – always teasing!' Calum complained.

The antique clock on the wall to their right chimed the first of ten chimes.

'OK, you two! That'll do!' Mr Truelove said sternly. 'I'm sure the boys saw something. I couldn't believe it when I found their fishing tackle abandoned . . . I know it would take something serious to make Calum do that!'

'Course they saw something, Dad!' Becky giggled. 'It's like I said before, "small boys – big imagination". It's those daft comics they read – about aliens and stuff!'

'How do *you* know what I read?' Calum snapped back. 'Have you been going through my magazines again?'

Becky sipped her drink and sneered over the rim of her cup. 'As *if* . . .'

'Why don't you two girls turn in?' Mrs Truelove suggested sternly. 'The boys can go up later when we've all calmed down.'

'Suits us,' Becky said defiantly. 'Come on, Sam. Let's leave the "ghost hunters" to it!'

'Don't be cheeky!' Mr Truelove shouted after her, as she and Sam climbed the wooden steps leading up to the bedrooms.

When the girls had gone, Mr Truelove turned to face Billy and Calum. 'Now look – I don't know what you saw out there, but, as I've just said, I do believe you saw *something.*'

'There's probably a perfectly logical explanation,' Mrs Truelove chipped in.

'No, Mum! I'm telling you – me and Billy really saw something . . . something very scary . . . like a ghost.'

'Calum, I'm sure that you *think* —' Mrs Truelove began sympathetically. But before she could finish, Billy, who so far had said very little, suddenly interrupted.

'*It was a Viking warrior!*'

Everyone turned and stared at him.

'It was a Viking warrior,' Billy repeated in a matter-of-fact way. 'I recognised the clothes, the sword and the helmet – most of all the helmet.'

'He's right, Dad,' Calum added. 'We've just done Vikings again at school.' He stared at Billy and looked thoughtful. 'And apart from the sword, what was that he was carrying in his other hand?'

'You mean the thing that looked like a string shopping bag?'

'Yes.'

Billy paused and sipped the dregs from his cup before he answered. Mr and Mrs Truelove waited for his reply just as intently as Calum.

'A head — a human head!' Billy said calmly. 'One of his victims.'

Mrs Truelove almost choked and jumped to her feet. 'Well, that's just about enough for tonight. Maybe Becky's right about small boys with big imaginations. Let's have you two off to bed.'

Ten minutes later, Billy and Calum were in their bunk beds chatting on about everything that had happened.

'I don't want to freak you out, Billy,' Calum said from the bottom bunk, 'but do you think that Viking ghost, or whatever it was, was after *you*? It seemed to be looking more at you than me.'

Billy stared up at the little square panel in the centre of the ceiling — there was no sound of movement. 'I don't know,' he shouted back down to Calum. 'But there's something else that's really weird — to do with that helmet.'

'It was scary!'

'I've seen it before.'

'Never! Where?'

Billy got out of bed and climbed down the ladder. He

went over to the pine dresser, opened the bottom drawer and pulled out the rolled-up paper.

Calum sat up as Billy knelt by the edge of his bunk. 'Is that the weird drawing you did in the art lesson?'

'Yes . . . I finished it at home, during the night. Only it wasn't me that was doing it . . . It was like someone else – sort of guiding me.'

'That sounds freaky, Billy. Let's have a look.'

Billy slowly unrolled the paper and spread it out in front of his friend. And then he watched as Calum's eyes grew wide and his mouth fell open. He'd never seen Calum look so dumbfounded in all the time they'd known each other.

'Oh my God!' Calum exclaimed. *'It's that helmet – with the mouth – exactly the same as the ghost was wearing!'*

A knock on the trapdoor made both their hearts leap. Billy quickly rolled up the paper. He climbed back into the top bunk and stuffed it under his pillow.

'It's only me,' said Mr Truelove, his head and shoulders sticking up above the trapdoor. 'Lights out now, please, and off to sleep . . . Try to put ghosts and phantom warriors and suchlike out of your minds. Goodnight!'

Calum switched off the lamp on the bedside table and the two boys snuggled under their duvets. Within minutes they'd dropped off to sleep.

And whilst they slept, the Fen Phantom waded through the margins of the dark fen, his huge body as cold as ice and stinking of stagnant water and stale blood. And he held up the rotting human

head to the moon above and screamed a fearful cry, rueing the day
he had flung the blind woman on to the rocks. But he knew it would
only be a matter of time before 'the final battle was fought'. He
would crush the young boy's puny bones and drive his remains deep
into the mud and silt that he, the mighty Sigurd, had been forced to
stalk this last thousand years!

15
Breakages

The following morning, Mr Truelove accompanied the boys to the dyke to retrieve their fishing tackle.

They surveyed the scene in total horror and bewilderment.

Everything had been ruthlessly trashed.

Mr Truelove picked up the rod he had loaned Billy. It had been snapped into two pieces – broken like a twig. In fact, lots of other items of tackle had been broken in the same way.

'Look, Dad!' Calum said, holding up the landing net. 'The handle's been snapped in two and all of the floats are broken in half.'

'Someone's got a sick sense of humour,' Mr Truelove grumbled.

Billy looked around in dismay.

Anything that wouldn't break cleanly had been bent, smashed or flattened. Even the little plastic bait containers had been emptied of maggots and shattered into small pieces.

'What you saw last night was no ghost,' Mr Truelove muttered. 'Someone very real did this.'

But Billy wasn't convinced.

In his own mind, the Viking warrior *was* real — at least in some ways, and yet in others *unreal* — like a ghost. But the most important thing, was that Billy was sure that what they had seen last night was *in all ways* extremely dangerous.

During breakfast everyone voted for what they wanted to do.

The weather was fine and fresh, the sun peeping through the clouds, but it was too cool to sit on the beach, so Mrs Truelove suggested that they might go and see a few of the local attractions. A glossy brochure entitled *What to See and Do in Great Yarmouth* was passed around the breakfast table and, in no time at all, everyone was making suggestions.

Mr Truelove took charge. 'OK, adults first. Anne — what would you like to do?'

Mrs Truelove paused from stacking the empty cereal bowls. 'Well, there's an old church I'd like to take a look at. It's only a short drive from here — down at Wickerdyke.'

Billy smiled to himself as Calum, Becky and Sam all gave disapproving looks and Calum whispered 'Boring!' under his breath.

'A very reasonable request,' Mr Truelove said. 'Now you kids, starting with Sam – what would you like to do?'

Sam wanted to visit the Sea Life Centre. Becky was more than happy to wander around the town browsing in the shops. Billy hesitantly requested that they took the broken fishing rods to the tackle shop to get them repaired. He felt guilty and offered to pay for his own out of his spending money.

'That's really kind of you to offer, Billy,' Mr Truelove said sympathetically. 'But I'll pay for the damage . . . It wasn't your fault.'

'And can we get some more bait, Dad?' Calum pleaded.

'You're never going to fish again, after what happened?' Mrs Truelove asked with a look of horror spreading across her face.

'Now calm down, Anne,' Mr Truelove replied. 'We might give it another go later in the week, but only on the main river – and I certainly won't be leaving the boys on their own again.'

'I should hope not,' Mrs Truelove muttered. 'I thought fishing was supposed to be a quiet, peaceful occupation.'

So did I, Billy thought to himself.

Fifteen minutes later, Billy was sitting on his bunk, looking through the small window out across the vast flatness of the marsh.

'Hey, Calum! Take a look at this.'

Calum climbed up on Billy's bunk, knelt by his side and looked out to where he was pointing. Two large, billowing sails seemed to be making their way across the distant fields. And further to the left was what looked like a tall ship's mast, but this was moving in the opposite direction.

'They look weird, don't they? It's the main river – the River Yare. It's right where you're pointing, It's just that you can't see the water for the tall reeds.'

Before Billy had chance to say anything else, a loud bang sounded from the loft space above their heads. Calum almost rolled off the bed.

'Ww-what was that?' he stammered. 'Hang on, Billy. I'm going to get Dad.'

But Mr Truelove had just arrived at the top of the wooden steps. 'What are you two playing at? We've been ready and waiting to go for the last five minutes!'

'Dad! There's something moving about in the loft again. It sounds really heavy.'

Mr Truelove sighed and glanced at his watch. 'Well, I'll just take a quick look, but I doubt if I'll be able to see anything without a lamp. It might be better to wait till we get back.'

Mr Truelove told the boys to climb down. He manhandled the beds directly under the loft panel and climbed on to the top bunk. He reached the ceiling easily and pushed the wooden panel back. Placing the bunk-bed ladder against the dark opening, he began to climb upwards.

'Be careful, Mr Truelove!' Billy said, feeling distinctly uncomfortable.

The light from the bedroom flooded up into the loft and illuminated the space around Mr Truelove, but otherwise everything was still in blackness.

'I can't see much – it's too dark. I suppose there could be some sort of creatures hiding there – mice, birds or bats or something.'

Mr Truelove was right. There was a creature hiding in the shadows and it was watching his every move.

'Dad, it was too heavy to be a mouse or a bat . . . It made a right racket, didn't it, Billy?'

Billy didn't answer. He suddenly felt the hairs on the back of his neck standing on end. Something wasn't right. He sensed that Mr Truelove was in danger.

'Leave it, Mr Truelove. We need to go – the others are shouting,' Billy lied.

And just as the creature braced itself, ready to strike at the infiltrator's most vulnerable point – his eyes – Mr Truelove withdrew.

'You're right. Let's leave it for now – I'll take another look later.'

And so the creature remained in the shadows, keeping quite still, until a few moments later the loft panel slid back into place and the bedroom underneath became quiet again.

16
Legend and Folklore

Billy and Calum walked into the tackle shop carrying their broken rods. It was Calum who saw the old man first; he was standing over on the far side of the shop chatting to a customer.

'Let's wait here,' Billy suggested. 'We can have another look at that big pike.'

But before they had chance, the man glanced across at them and walked over. Billy noticed for the first time that the old man walked in a very curious way, stooped over and limping. 'And what would you two be after?' the man asked, his eyes firmly fixed on Billy's rod bag.

'Our rods got broken and we were wondering if you could fix them?'

The man took the rod bag from Billy and then looked at the two friends with a very serious expression. 'Aren't you two staying up at Fenthorpe — you were in here with your dad yesterday morning?'

'That was *my* dad, not his,' Calum stated. 'But yes — we came in yesterday.'

The man focused his attention back on the bag and took out the two halves of the broken rod. His face turned a funny colour — a sort of greyish-white. 'Dare I ask what happened to this?' he enquired, almost accusingly.

'You wouldn't believe it!' Billy replied confidently.

'Did you fish Demon's Dyke?'

Calum began to fidget. It was Billy who replied. 'Yes!'

'Well then, I'd believe anything! Didn't I tell you to stick to the main river?' His voice trembled a little. He took Calum's rod but didn't examine it. 'Wait here!'

He disappeared into the back of the shop and reappeared a few moments later with a slip of paper. 'Here's a receipt for the rods. They'll be ready day after tomorrow.'

'Thanks,' Billy said, taking the piece of paper and folding it into his jeans pocket, 'but don't you want to know what happened to—'

'Look!' The man cut Billy off mid-sentence and lowered his voice to a whisper. 'I don't want to know! Just stay away from the dykes! See you on Thursday.'

As soon as Billy and Calum were outside the shop, they stared at each other wide-eyed.

'What was all that about?' Calum asked.

'I don't know,' Billy answered. 'He was certainly acting a bit weird.'

Calum nodded. 'Never mind. I'm hungry. Come on – let's go and meet the others in the Winter Gardens.'

After a cloudy afternoon spent wandering around the town the people-carrier pulled up outside a lonely church on the edge of the Wickerdyke marshes.

The band of holidaymakers stepped out and was immediately aware of the overwhelming stillness.

'It's very remote out here, isn't it?' Mr Truelove said, scanning around.

Apart from an ancient-looking farm and a few thatched cottages across from the church, there were no signs of habitation. The narrow lane they'd driven down came to an abrupt end by the church gate, where a vast flat vista of narrow ditches, dykes and marshes stretched out in all directions. The late-afternoon sun made a welcome appearance, but a thick mist was rapidly forming and settling over the eerie landscape.

Mrs Truelove was already on her way up the stone-flagged path heading towards the ancient-looking arched doorway. 'I hope it's open,' she called back.

Billy and Calum followed, the two girls sauntering behind. Mr Truelove locked the car.

'It's spooky out here, Billy. This church looks seriously old,' Calum whispered.

Billy nodded.

Mrs Truelove managed to turn the heavy iron latch and the door creaked open. As Billy moved up behind her, a strange odour filled his nostrils – a mixture of stale air and furniture polish.

Mrs Truelove stepped forward through the doorway and almost jumped back in surprise. 'Oh good gracious! Just look at this!'

Billy and Calum edged past her to see what she'd spotted.

There, on the opposite wall was an enormous wallpainting. Billy and Calum gasped at the sight of it. It depicted three kings alongside three grotesque skeletons. The medieval figures stretched from halfway up the church wall almost to the ceiling.

'That looks so creepy,' Calum exclaimed.

Mrs Truelove picked up an information sheet and began reading it. 'An ancient legend depicts three kings who, while hunting in the forest, come upon three corpses – which they discover to be their own.'

Becky, Sam and Mr Truelove had now made their way into the church and were listening to Mrs Truelove's commentary as they stared up at the painting.

'What's the point of it?' Becky asked, in her usual sulky way.

'Give me a chance,' Mrs Truelove replied without taking her eyes off the leaflet. 'Well, according to this – it seems

that "the painting is an allegory impressing on us the transitory nature of life".'

'Oh well! That's very clear,' Becky said, with as much sarcasm as she could muster.

Mrs Truelove ignored her and continued: 'The message of the corpses, or skeletons, is this:

As you are now, so once were we
As we are now, so shall you be

'So I think the point it's trying to make, is that no one is alive for very long – that the time between living and dying is very short. I suppose it's all a bit morbid, really.'

Billy found himself fascinated by Mrs Truelove's words. The whole thing seemed to hold some sort of special significance for him – and yet he wasn't sure what it was.

'OK then!' Mr Truelove broke the sombre silence. 'Why don't we all go to different parts of the church and see who can come up with the most interesting artefact?'

'What's an artefact?' Billy whispered to Calum.

Calum shrugged his shoulders. 'I haven't a clue. Come on – let's see what we can find.'

Billy looked up again at the three grinning skeletons and felt a shiver run down his spine, and then he moved off towards the front of the church – where Calum had already spotted a pair of crumbling stone tombs.

Just by the side of the tombs, two red velvet curtains divided off a small room. Billy peeped through them into the semi-darkness, whilst Calum read the inscriptions on the tombs.

'This guy was the Bailiff of Yarmouth in 1271,' Calum informed him. But Billy was far more interested in what lay on the other side of the curtains. He slipped through the gap, found an old-fashioned light switch on the wall and flicked it on. A single, low-powered electric light bulb lit up the small space – and Billy shrieked out and reeled backwards as he saw the image on the wall in front of him.

Calum was the first to arrive by his side, closely followed by the two girls, and finally by Mr and Mrs Truelove.

They all stood in a huddle and stared silently up at the chancel wall.

Another ancient wallpainting: this time a huge warrior-like figure holding a smaller figure by the ankle and dangling it upside down like a rag-doll. Around the warrior lay other smaller figures, their bodies crumpled, arms and legs crooked and bent awkwardly. There were a few other people in the foreground – in the act of running away, their faces contorted and twisted in terror.

As everyone continued to stare in awe at the awful picture, a voice from behind broke the silence and startled everyone.

'*Would you be liking ghost stories?*'

Billy swivelled round to see a small stocky man creep out of the shadows. He was wearing a strange type of flat cap on top of his round plump head. He stood with his hands deep in the pockets of a pair of scruffy trousers, tied carelessly with a thick leather belt.

'You're obviously from round here?' Mr Truelove stated and asked at the same time.

'That'll be right. I'm the church caretaker – just arrived to lock up for the night. But there's no hurry. We're always happy to see a few travellers about the place – though, strictly speaking, this part of the church is reserved for the vicar.'

'Sorry!' Mrs Truelove apologised, colouring up slightly.

'No need to apologise,' the old caretaker replied. 'And now that you've discovered the Fen Phantom you'll be wanting to know a bit more, I suppose?'

At the mention of 'Fen Phantom' Billy tensed and stared at the old man. 'Is he real? And why is he holding that other man upside down?'

The old man's mouth broke into a smile, allowing numerous wrinkles to crease his weathered face. 'Well, in answer to your first question, there's them that believe he did exist – a fierce Viking warrior with a terrible reputation. But now then, I don't want to be giving you kids nightmares.'

'You won't!' Calum said, his curiosity aroused much the same as everyone else's. 'Please carry on.'

The old man shuffled up to the wallpainting and stared upwards. 'Well in answer to the young man's second question, he's holding that poor wretch upside down and about to snap his leg – just like all those others piled around him. According to the legend, they've all got broken bones – can you see how their legs is all twisted?'

'Yuck – it's disgusting!' Becky protested, turning to Sam and pulling a face. 'Come on – I've heard enough of this . . . Let's wait in the car.'

Mr Truelove frowned, fumbled in his pocket and passed the car keys to his daughter.

'Why is he called the Fen Phantom?' Mrs Truelove asked.

'Cos there's a good few people round here believes that the Viking's ghost haunts these marshes – especially around Fenthorpe. Have you visited there yet?'

'We're staying at Fenthorpe,' Calum stated, his voice full of nervous excitement. 'We're staying in an old windmill.'

'Well I never!' The old man took off his cap and scratched the top of his bald head. 'I thought the old windmill was still empty. The owner said he'd never rent it out again after what happened five years ago – said it wasn't worth the trouble.'

Billy saw the expression of alarm spread across Mr Truelove's face. 'Why? What happened?'

But the old man was reluctant to say any more. He took an old pocket watch from the breast pocket of his worn waistcoat and looked at it. 'I'm sorry, but it's high time I was locking up and getting back for my tea. If you want to know more, then I suggest you contact the windmill's owner. And would you believe he happens to be an expert on that there painting. In fact he knows more than anybody about local history and things like that. Anyway, I really need to be on my way now – my missus will be wondering where I've got to.'

Whilst the old man jangled a huge bunch of heavy keys, they took a last look at the sinister painting and sauntered over to the door, everyone deep in thought. But no one said anything until they were all back in the car.

'It's too much of a coincidence, what with the boys seeing what they thought was a ghost, and then that business in there about the Fen Phantom. Something strange is definitely going on. In fact, things seem to be getting weirder by the minute.'

'Incredible – those boys have got Mum ranting on now,' Becky sighed. 'It's all a load of rubbish if you ask me – it's just stupid stories.'

'Well nobody did ask you!' Calum snapped.

Becky scowled and put her tongue out.

But Mr Truelove was too busy to notice. He was rooting around in the glove compartment. 'It's here!' he finally said in triumph. 'The holiday directions, complete with a copy of the booking form.'

'Fenland Holidays, isn't it? I remember phoning them,' Mrs Truelove stated, looking over his shoulder.

'Yes, but the telephone number and address of the owner are here – a Mr Titus Fenn of Fenthorpe Grange. That's the big mansion-type house that we drove past. I might just give him a call tomorrow. I'd like to know what happened in the windmill five years ago and why he's suddenly decided to rent it again.'

As Mr Truelove started the engine and the car pulled away, Billy took a last look back at the church. He saw the caretaker walking down the pathway and then, from somewhere up on the church roof, a huge black bird took off into the air and disappeared in the rapidly thickening mist.

17
Titus fen

It was Wednesday morning.

Billy had slept deeply and woke up in the room alone.
Calum and the rest of the family were already downstairs,
seated around the breakfast table. Billy got up, threw on his
clothes and crept downstairs to join them. As he walked into
the kitchen, a ring-tone sounded and Mr Truelove put his
mobile to his ear.

'Hi, Billy!' Calum said in his usual friendly way. 'We
thought we'd let you have a lie-in this morning, especially as
the weather's turned foul. It's pouring with rain outside.'

Billy looked towards one of the small windows. The rain
splattered against the glass and ran down the pane in
streams. 'I see what you mean.'

'Billy – your mum's on the phone . . . She's desperate to
talk to you,' Mr Truelove interrupted.

Billy thanked him, reached over, took the mobile and moved away from the table.

'Billy-boy! Is that you?'

'Hi, Mum.'

'How are you, Billy? Is everything OK?'

'Sort of . . .'

'What do you mean, "sort of"? Is everything *really* OK?'

'You sound worried, Mum!'

'That's just the point, Billy. I *am* worried! I've been having some strange dreams . . .'

'What do you mean?'

'Bethan, Billy – a woman called Bethan . . . I've seen her in my dreams.'

'Who's Bethan?'

There was a pause before Billy's mum replied. 'It sounds crazy, Billy, but she's a distant relative – one of our ancestors. She was killed by a warrior.'

Billy felt a shiver run down his spine. 'It wouldn't be a Viking warrior, would it?'

'Billy – how did—'

'Just carry on, Mum.'

'The letter "S" in the tealeaves, Billy. Do you remember? "S" for "special"!'

'Yes, Mum. I remember!'

His mum paused again. Billy braced himself for what was coming next.

'Well it wasn't "S" for "special", Billy — it was "S" for "Sigurd".'

'Mum — I don't understand.'

'Look, Billy — there's something weird going on. You've got to keep in touch. I'm worried . . .'

Billy knew if he wanted the holiday to continue, he would have to reassure his mum. 'We're having a great time. Honest. I only said "Viking" because we've just studied them at school, and me and Calum have been talking about them a lot recently.'

Another pause. 'Billy — I'm really worried. You must keep in touch. I mean it! If you don't, I promise I'll catch the first train down there!'

'But, Mum—'

'No buts, Billy! Hand the phone back to Mr Truelove and I'll have a word with him. And make sure you stick close to Calum and his family — promise me, Billy!'

Billy felt sorry for his mum. There was a lot of agitation in her voice and she had every right to be concerned. She'd sensed that something odd was happening and he wasn't really in a position to argue.

'OK, Mum — I promise. I'll pass you back to Mr Truelove.'

Billy passed the phone back to Calum's dad.

Mr Truelove and Billy's mum chatted on the phone, and all went quiet around the breakfast table. Billy poured some cereal into a bowl and tried to behave as normally as possible. He felt embarrassed about his mum checking up on him.

Mr Truelove finally switched off his phone and looked across the table. 'Your mum asked me to make sure you ring her more often, Billy. And she wouldn't mind a postcard if you've got time. She said something about Beth missing you, but secretly I suspect it's your mum that's missing you the most.'

'Ah – poor little Billy! And I bet he's missing his mummy too. He's been having nightmares about the big bad ghost!' Becky teased, much to Sam's amusement.

Mr and Mrs Truelove both glowered at her.

'Leave him alone! We *did* see something – why won't you believe us?' Calum shouted up in Billy's defence.

Billy said nothing. He ate his cornflakes and hoped that no one would notice that his hand was beginning to shake a little.

The weather forecast predicted thunderstorms in the morning and clearer, sunny intervals in the afternoon. And so, much to Becky and Sam's annoyance, Mr Truelove suggested that they drop in at Fenthorpe Grange and pay Titus Fenn a visit.

Mrs Truelove was very much in agreement. She was keen to learn a bit more about the local history of the area, and Mr Truelove was curious to find out about the incident at their windmill five years ago.

As for Billy and Calum — they couldn't believe their luck! They were more than keen to visit the spooky house and hopefully find out a bit more about the Fen Phantom.

Mr Truelove made the necessary phone call, and Titus Fenn warmly accepted his request and invited them all for coffee. The visit was arranged for eleven o'clock.

After some argument it was finally agreed that the girls could stay behind at the windmill and listen to their CDs. Mr Truelove was reluctant, but his wife insisted that the girls could be trusted.

It was just after eleven o'clock when the people-carrier cruised through the massive stone pillars of Fenthorpe Grange, crunched its way down the gravel drive and pulled up in front of two large stone dogs guarding the steps and entrance to the impressive mansion. Although it was mid-morning, it felt more like late evening: the sky was black and the daylight had almost faded to nothing.

Billy was the first to get out of the car. He stared around and took in the building's exterior, scanning the Gothic architecture with wide eyes.

The grey stone walls were dotted with numerous arched windows; he noticed that a few of the larger downstairs windows were dimly lit by shimmering lights.

He craned his neck and stared up at the gabled rooftops, bordered with ferocious stone gargoyles, and to the towering chimneys reaching up to the leaden sky.

As he looked away, he saw something out of the corner of his eye — something big and black — by one of the chimneys . . . And then it was gone. Was it that bird again? If so, why was it following him? Perhaps it was just his imagination playing tricks.

Mr Truelove led the way up the stone steps towards the arched wooden door. But before he had chance to knock, it creaked open and a woman asked them to step inside.

'Come on in! The professor's expecting you.'

Billy lingered a little, fascinated by the large stone dogs on either side of the top step. Just before the woman closed the door, he glanced back and froze as one of the dogs' eyes seemed to follow him.

No! They couldn't have moved! He was jumpy and his imagination was definitely playing tricks!

Once inside the entrance hall, the small party found themselves overwhelmed by the strange grandeur of their surroundings. It was like stepping inside an Aladdin's Cave, full of bizarre and intriguing objects — like some kind of vast museum.

'This way, if you will,' the woman requested, in a strong Norfolk accent.

She led them out of the huge entrance hall and down an oak-panelled corridor lined with suits of armour. The walls were adorned with portraits and pictures, all pertaining to scenes of ancient battles and war. As Billy looked up at them, the scenes came to life; the small figures animated, battling each other – he could almost hear their cries . . .

Billy began to fill with panic. He was definitely feeling strange. As his footsteps rang out on the polished wooden floor, he found himself growing more nervous by the second.

'Come on in – I've been expecting you!'

The man was sitting in a large winged chair with his back to them. He was facing the most amazing fireplace Billy had ever seen. A great log fire blazed in between two flat stone pillars bridged by an enormous dark wood mantle. Warrior-like figures were carved into the pillars, linked together in some sort of spiral pattern.

Above the wooden mantle, two savage-looking battle-axes hung on the wall. They crossed each other and glistened in the firelight. The only other light was from the numerous candles placed in ornate candlesticks by each of the leaded windows. Billy realised that these were the source of the shimmering lights he'd seen from outside.

As the figure rose out of the chair and slowly turned to face them, Calum gasped, Mr and Mrs Truelove coughed politely, and Billy almost choked.

'It's a pleasure to meet you – come over by the fire and take a seat. Clarice, bring our guests some drinks. Tea? Coffee? Fruit juice, perhaps, for the boys?'

Billy had never seen a real-life vampire before, but if they really existed, then the figure in front of them was definitely a vampire.

'Titus Fenn?' Mr Truelove stepped forward and reached out to shake his hand.

'That's me, and Clarice tells me that you are the Truelove family – apart from the boy. Ah yes – Billy. I've been waiting for you for a long time – longer than you would ever imagine.'

Billy swallowed hard and gawped uncontrollably at the alarming appearance of the 'Dracula' standing in front of him.

Even stooping forward, Titus Fenn was very tall. His hair was jet-black, receding at the front and greased back in true vampire style. The pointed face looked pale, the skin almost white – in complete contrast to the piercing dark eyes. His clothes complemented his dark image: everything slim-fitting and black.

Without ever taking his eyes off Billy, the professor shook Mr Truelove's hand.

'How come you seem to know our son's friend, Mr Fenn?'

The stooping crow-like figure sat down and finally took his eyes off Billy. He replied in a slow, deep tone, 'Please call me "Professor". "Mr Fenn" sounds ridiculous.'

'What's your subject, Professor?' Mrs Truelove spoke up for the first time, genuine curiosity in her voice.

'He's a professor of ancient history – University of Norwich for more than fifteen years,' Clarice answered for him, shuffling in with a tray of drinks. 'Titus is one very clever man, but he would never admit to it.'

The professor smiled and stared into the fire. He reclined back in his chair, placed his hands together, intertwined his fingers and closed his eyes.

'In answer to your question, Mr Truelove, I don't know Billy – at least not in the physical sense. However, I am acquainted with him in other ways most intimately. Our paths were always destined to cross and I have waited patiently for this moment – for a good number of years, in fact.'

Billy sipped his orange and looked around the room, his mind beginning to whirl. Everything had become so surreal. It was like being in a film set on TV, surrounded by actors – but he didn't belong there and he didn't know what to say, he didn't know his lines!

He looked across to Calum. He too wore a bewildered expression and obviously felt the same way. They both sipped their drinks and stared at each other, whilst Mr and Mrs Truelove looked uncomfortable and fidgeted nervously.

Before anyone had chance to speak, a flash of lightning lit up one of the windows. Seconds later a loud clap of thunder caused the sugar bowl and spoons to rattle on the tray that Clarice had left by the fire.

One of the candles snuffed out, so that the overall effect was extremely creepy.

The professor, still reclined back with his eyes closed, had remained as still as a statue. Just as everyone thought he'd fallen asleep, the dark piercing eyes flashed open and he turned towards Billy.

'Can you feel his presence, Billy – the giant Viking warrior? He's waiting for you!'

18
Creeping Shadows

Billy began to feel faint. His face felt hot and cold at the same time.

'Have you felt a presence around you, Billy – as if you're being watched?'

Billy nodded solemnly, fidgeted in his seat and clung tight to his glass of orange.

Calum and his parents looked on in awe as the professor leant forward and continued almost in a whisper: 'A shadow for much of the time, Billy, a demon trapped between two worlds – the real world as he used to know it, and a world of dark shadows. And his shadow looms over you even as we speak.'

Billy felt himself breaking out in a cold sweat.

'You're frightening the boy,' Mr Truelove said in a harsh tone. 'What do you mean by "demon"? Which demon?'

'The Viking warrior,' the professor replied without taking his eyes off Billy. 'The one who drew you here.'

Mr Truelove placed his cup and saucer back on the tray and his expression changed to one of impatience. 'That's ridiculous! Nobody drew us here. We came of our own free will and we just happened to invite Billy along, to join us on holiday.'

'I'm afraid that nothing "just happens", Mr Truelove — every event and action that takes place in this universe is decreed by forces that neither you nor I have the power to understand or contradict. Believe me, you and your family were instrumental in delivering Billy to his destiny. He has to avenge the great wrong that befell his ancestors hundreds of years ago.'

A hush fell across the room. Only the sound of the logs cracking and spitting on the fire broke the silence. Billy tried to take in the professor's words, as Calum and his parents stared across at him. His head began to spin again and this time he dropped his glass of orange on to the floor.

Mrs Truelove rushed over to him. 'Steady, Billy! Take no notice.' She looked over to her husband and shouted angrily, 'Come on — we're leaving!'

'We saw something on the marshes the other night,' Calum suddenly blurted out to the professor. 'It was like a phantom warrior. Would that be the demon you're talking about?'

'Ah — so you've seen him already! His penance is to stalk the marshes. You were lucky to escape unharmed.'

Mrs Truelove frowned in the direction of the professor, as he stood up and continued: 'I stopped renting the windmill some years ago. A boy and girl – brother and sister – were on holiday with their parents. The two of them were on the footpath near Bickerdyke Fen. They were out late, on their own – they shouldn't have been. I'd warned their parents of the dangers – they'd just laughed, labelled me as an eccentric old fool. The Fen Phantom, as the locals call him, appeared from under the bridge. The children fled screaming towards Ferryman's Lane, but it was too late. The boy got away, but the girl was found later that night face-down in the dyke. Of course the authorities disbelieved the boy's incredible story. A simple case of misadventure, they said.'

'Oh my God! That's awful!' Mrs Truelove said, putting her hands to her face.

'I didn't believe the stories myself at first,' the professor went on. 'I began researching the Bonebreaker legend about ten years ago, convinced it was nothing more than folklore. But then a friend of mine, a lecturer at the university, got me interested in the paranormal. Suddenly, myth and legend turned into horrifying reality. Consequently my research became more and more obsessive. It turned out that over the years there have been lots of incidents. More recently, Tom Walters—'

'The man in the tackle shop!' Calum exclaimed.

'What happened to him?' Mr Truelove asked.

'He was out fishing, on his own, close to where Demon's

Dyke meets the main river. He was doing quite well and fished on after dark. And then the light came upon him.'

'A bright light, sort of yellow and blue – we saw it, Billy and me,' Calum said nervously.

'Only you got away – Tom Walters didn't. He was found unconscious the following morning. Both his legs were broken.'

Billy sat with his head in his hands. He remembered seeing the way that Tom Walters had limped across the shop. What sort of creature could do that to a harmless old man?

Mr Truelove yelled at the professor, 'But why rent us the windmill if the place is so dangerous?'

'I'm sorry. I had no choice. Your destiny is to be here – with Billy.' The professor looked across at Mrs Truelove. 'If the boy is well enough to stand on his feet, then I would like you all to follow me.'

Mrs Truelove cast a concerned glance at Billy.

'I'm fine, Mrs Truelove,' Billy said, reading her mind.

The professor walked towards another doorway in the corner of the room and beckoned everyone to follow.

He led them into what looked like a huge dining room. An enormous rectangular table, complete with regency-style chairs, took up most of the space, but it was the gigantic painting on the far wall that drew everyone's eyes.

The terrifying figure, masked with a ferocious helmet, stood at least seven-feet-tall and dwarfed the two warriors by his side. In the background, over the tops of tall reeds, people could be seen fleeing from the raiders' swords; whilst in the foreground, the huge Viking towered over his unfortunate victims, their prostrate bodies lying twisted amongst the mud and reed-stems. In one hand he wielded a mighty sword, but the worst and most gruesome thing was the item he carried carelessly in the other – a human head.

The horrific image was difficult to come to terms with. Its impact was mind-blowing – the stuff of nightmares!

Billy recognised it at once as the Viking warrior that had interrupted their fishing expedition.

The professor stood with his arms folded and stared up at the figure, almost as if in admiration. Finally, with his audience still looking on in shocked silence, he directed his gaze towards Billy.

'So there he is, Billy, the demon that stalks your dreams and your wakefulness. He was head of the dreaded Berserkers – the most feared of all the Viking armies. They had no respect for life or limb; they would whip themselves up into a frenzy and slaughter every living creature in sight. There are stories that they even killed each other. *And this man was more evil than you would ever believe.*'

The atmosphere in the room grew more and more tense as the professor continued.

'His chosen method of slaying his victims was to pick them up by the legs, like a rag-doll, and offer them up to his god, Odin. He would break their bones and dump them on the ground, leaving them to die slowly. His infamous reputation spread quickly so that he became the most feared warrior of his time – he was known as Sigurd the Bonebreaker!'

Sigurd! The name his mum had mentioned on the phone!

Billy felt himself fill with panic. He started to feel much more faint. The room began to spin as thoughts and images swirled around in his mind – the flickering candles; the oak-panelled walls; the gabled roofs; the black shape by the chimney; the stone dog's eyes following him; the horrific figure of the Bonebreaker looming over him; the human head hanging from his fist, bloodied with lifeless staring eyes – all these images going round and round in Billy's head . . . merging into a blurry nightmare . . . and then . . . *all-enveloping blackness.*

Billy hit the floor in a crumpled heap!

When Billy came round, a wrinkled vampire-face stared down at him.

'Billy! How do you feel?'

Billy looked into the professor's eyes. He thought he was still dreaming. Slowly, his mind cleared and he saw that he was back in the room with the big log fire, stretched out on the sofa. The professor was stooping over him; Calum knelt on the floor by his side.

'What happened? How long . . . ?'

'Now just stay calm, Billy,' the professor said, leaning closer. 'Everything's going to be OK. You fainted.'

Billy dragged himself up on to his elbows. He saw that he was covered by a duvet and still wearing his clothes.

'I told the professor all about the weird things that have been happening,' Calum said enthusiastically. 'He knows everything.'

'I'm still not sure about any of this,' Mr Truelove said from somewhere in the background.

The professor placed a cool slender hand on Billy's forehead. 'You're very hot. You need to rest. You're going to need all your strength if we're going to stand a chance of beating this demon.'

Billy felt the panic beginning to well up in his stomach again. 'What do you mean *we*? Isn't it *me* he's after? And anyway, why me in the first place?'

'This is ridiculous!' Mr Truelove spoke up, his voice full of concern. 'How can an eleven-year-old child be involved with a Viking warrior?'

'Because Billy is a very special eleven-year-old,' the professor replied calmly. 'He is the direct descendant of Wilfrid, a Saxon boy who lived in the ninth century.'

Once more, a silence ensued – just the occasional spitting and hissing of burning logs before the professor continued. 'A Viking raiding party plundered the boy's village and the heathens showed no mercy. Those who failed to escape were killed, slaughtered – just a few were spared and kept as slaves.'

Mrs Truelove took a step forward and sat on the far end of

the sofa at Billy's feet. 'And what about Wilfrid?' she asked.

'By a miracle, he survived – unlike his mother.'

'Bethan!' Billy exclaimed.

'You know her name?' the professor uttered in surprise.

Billy began to shake with nervous excitement. 'Not really – it's just that Mum told me she's been having some strange dreams ... getting messages from someone called Bethan.'

'Your mother has no doubt inherited the soothsayer's psychic powers.'

The professor stood up, clasped his hands and stared into space. 'Bethan was Wilfrid's mother. She was blind. The Bonebreaker flung her mercilessly over the cliffs after she'd put a curse on the Viking demon.'

'And this curse,' Mrs Truelove chipped in, 'what was it exactly?'

The professor looked back at her with a stare of frightening intensity. 'Wilfrid's mother decreed that the Bonebreaker's soul should stalk the marshes until such time that one of her descendants would exact revenge.'

'What happened to the Bonebreaker, after he'd been cursed?' Billy asked, his voice trembling with anticipation.

'There is evidence to suggest that Sigurd moved on to York and caused havoc in the raids on the city. An archaeologist friend of mine believes that he may have died there. The search still goes on for his burial place.' The professor's eyes blazed with excitement. 'Imagine unearthing a seven-foot skeleton!'

'And what about Wilfrid?' Calum asked. 'What happened to him?'

'The story is that he rebuilt the village and became a great Saxon leader. He became known as "Wilfrid the Invincible".'

Mr Truelove stood up and began pacing around. 'And you really think that young Billy here is Wilfrid's direct descendant?'

'Quite right! I firmly believe that Billy and his mother echo the very existence of Wilfrid and Bethan. And now Billy must face the grim task of avenging the terrible wrong that was done to Wilfrid's mother and his people.'

'Tell them about the bird, Billy!' Calum said, nudging Billy's shoulder.

'Yes, please do,' the professor requested, his eyes glancing from Calum to Billy.

Trying hard to stop his voice from trembling, Billy told the professor about the strange incident back home involving his bedroom window, and the other sightings of the sinister black bird.

'Skallagrim!' the professor announced without hesitation. 'Skallagrim was the raven that accompanied the Bonebreaker throughout his devilish raids. The bird was a highly trained spy, seeking out victims and relaying their whereabouts with its demonic cries.'

'So animals and birds have direct descendants, like people?' Billy said, looking thoughtful.

'Of course! What are you thinking, Billy?'

'That bird — Skallagrim . . . I think I know where to find it — er, I mean its descendant . . .'

As Billy spoke, he looked at Calum and Calum looked back, his mouth slowly falling open as the realisation of what Billy was suggesting finally sank in.

'Blimey!' Calum gasped. 'The raven — it's in the windmill, living in the loft!'

19
making Contact

It was getting dark as Mr Truelove's people-carrier drew up outside the windmill, the professor pulling up close behind in an old ex-army Landrover.

Billy and Calum looked curiously at each other as Becky and Sam ran up to the car, panting for breath.

'Thank God you're back!' Becky gasped. 'The lights in the windmill won't switch on. In fact I think the power's off completely.'

'And we heard some funny fluttering noises coming from the rooms up above,' Sam joined in.

'And that's when we came outside to try and phone you on my mobile – but I couldn't get a signal . . . And then you pulled up – thank goodness!'

'OK! Calm down, we're here now,' Mr Truelove said reassuringly. He looked straight towards the professor, and then to Calum and Billy.

Billy knew at once what he was thinking – *the raven!*

They all moved away from the car and stood huddled under the deepening shadow of the windmill. Billy looked up at the sails silhouetted against the rapidly darkening sky. He felt he was being watched – that *they* were being watched . . . A shiver rattled down his spine.

'There're some candles in one of the kitchen drawers,' Mrs Truelove said.

'I've got a kerosene lamp in the Landrover – I'll go and get it,' the professor added.

Mr Truelove started back towards the people-carrier. 'And I'll get my big torch. Wait here. I'll only be a minute.'

Nobody argued. Nobody wanted to go inside. Billy wasn't sure he wanted to go in at all.

Ten minutes later, the kitchen was lit – more brightly at the centre, where the professor had suspended a kerosene lamp above the large circular table. Mrs Truelove placed the candles (there were only three of them) on the worktops. The cooker ran off a gas bottle, so they could at least prepare food and make hot drinks.

The professor, with the aid of Mr Truelove's torch, checked the fuse box tucked away at the back of a kitchen cupboard. 'The fuses are OK,' he informed everyone. 'It must be a power cut. They're pretty common around these parts. We'll give it half an hour and then I'll phone the electricity board.'

Billy, who had found himself constantly watching the professor's expressions and reactions, noted that he looked thoughtful as he spoke – as if he might be hiding something, not being completely honest.

'Come on,' the professor said to Mr Truelove, 'we ought to have a look around upstairs. We'll check that everything's secure.'

Billy and Calum insisted on accompanying them.

When they reached the top-floor bedroom, Billy pointed above his bed to show the professor the source of the noise that had previously disturbed them. Sure enough, Mr Truelove's torch beam revealed that the loft panel was slightly open – as if something had recently moved it.

The professor advised against going into the loft – too dangerous. They would be too vulnerable. It was dark enough outside the loft, never mind inside!

'That bird's been following us around ever since we arrived,' Billy announced. 'I saw it at your house, hiding behind the chimney.'

'Still keeping the enemy informed,' the professor sighed. 'Incredible that a bird can assist an evil spirit! I would like to suggest that for the time being nobody sleeps up here. We can bolt the trapdoor and seal this room off.'

Billy and Calum keenly nodded their approval.

'Now let's go down and join the others. We need to make plans – discuss our next move.'

Mr Truelove shone his powerful torch back towards the wooden steps leading down through the trapdoor. 'The professor's right. Come on – you first, Billy. Let's get out of here.'

'And I'll take up the rear,' the professor added, still peering cautiously up at the loft panel.

The procession moved warily down the steps. Mr Truelove paused and shone his torch back so that the professor could fasten the bolt and secure the trapdoor.

A few minutes later, they were back in the welcome light of the kitchen. Mrs Truelove had already prepared hot drinking chocolate and everyone sat around the kitchen table and sipped in silent contemplation.

It was Calum who finally broke the silence. 'Professor, you said the bird was real. Is the Viking real?'

The professor took a sip from his mug before replying, 'Yes and no. As I said earlier, the Bonebreaker is trapped between two worlds – the real world and a world of shadows. And there he must stay until Billy frees him.'

Billy almost choked on his chocolate. 'But I don't want to free him,' he spluttered.

'You have no choice, Billy,' the professor said with some sympathy in his voice. 'But don't forget – after the battle has been fought, this land will be freed from his evil presence forever.'

Mr Truelove spoke next. 'If the Viking isn't real, then how come he smashed up our fishing gear? And what about all those people he hurt in the past?'

The professor's eyes flashed around the table before resting on Mr Truelove. 'I didn't say he wasn't real. I said that he is trapped between two worlds. Out there on the marsh, his world is very real. He is still subject to the laws of the physical universe – as dangerous there as he ever was. Breaking Billy's tackle like that was a warning, a sign – broken in the same way he used to break bones.'

'But we're safe in here, aren't we?' Calum piped up. 'I mean, this windmill didn't even exist in Viking times, so this must be part of his shadowy world – so if he came here he would just be a harmless ghost, wouldn't he?'

'Almost right, young man!' the professor beamed. 'You're beginning to understand – though I would never label the Bonebreaker harmless. Phantoms are still capable of inflicting a great deal of psychological damage.'

Billy frowned and placed his empty mug on the table. 'What's "psychological"?'

'It means that it can have an effect on your mind, Billy,' Mr Truelove replied.

'Yeah . . .' Calum added, sneering towards his sister, 'some people are even spooked when the lights don't work.'

Billy watched as Becky scowled back at her brother and stuck her tongue out.

Before anyone could say anything else, Mr Truelove's mobile sent out a familiar ring-tone. No one spoke as he put it to his ear. 'OK, Mrs Hardacre . . . He's right here . . . I'll put him on.' He passed the phone to Billy. 'It's your mother, Billy. She sounds anxious.'

Billy took the phone and moved away from the table.

'Hi, Mum. I was going to ring you later.'

'Never mind that, Billy! Listen! You're in danger!'

His mother's voice sounded weak and crackly. The signal was beginning to break up.

'Why? What's wrong?'

'That woman I dreamt about—'

'Bethan?'

'Yes! I dreamt about her again, last night. She told me that the Viking is waiting for you, Billy.'

Billy felt a knot form in his stomach. His mother paused – he thought the signal had gone – and then she was back. 'It sounds incredible, but I believe it. I always knew you were special, Billy, and now . . .'

Billy strained to hear. The signal was breaking up again. 'Mum, I can't hear you. Can you hear me?'

The voice returned again, but this time hardly audible, all the time becoming weaker. 'Billy . . . phase . . . moon . . .'

'It's no good. You're breaking up, Mum.'

And then the signal went completely.

Billy returned to the table and passed the phone back to Mr Truelove.

'Is your mum OK, Billy?' Mrs Truelove asked.

'She's worried, really worried. She says I'm in danger.'

'I think you already know that, Billy,' the professor said, beckoning him to sit down at the table. At the same moment, the kerosene lamp dimmed and made a strange gurgling sound.

'I think the lamp's running out of oil, Professor,' Mr Truelove said.

The professor clasped his hands together and placed them on the table. He stared up at the light as it dimmed further. 'I think not, Mr Truelove. There is nothing physically wrong with that light. And I doubt there is anything wrong with the electricity supply. There are more powerful forces at work here. Can't you feel the atmosphere closing in on us?'

A stunned silence fell around the table. The professor continued to stare up at the lamp as he spoke. 'Billy is being drawn towards his destiny. The time is nigh for him to face the wrath of the Bonebreaker.'

Billy's stomach began to churn and he started to feel sick.

'But Billy *will* survive this, Professor, won't he? That goes without saying,' Mr Truelove claimed, indignantly.

'Nothing goes without saying, Mr Truelove. The only definite outcome of this confrontation will be that the Bonebreaker will subsequently depart his earthly existence and enter the spirit realm where he truly belongs. He believes this to be where Odin, his own god, resides. But who knows? Perhaps his spirit will disappear into the depths of Hell.'

Nobody could quite take in what the professor was saying – least of all Billy.

'So you see,' the professor went on, 'the outcome can only be for the better . . .'

Mr Truelove rose to his feet, anger welling up in his voice. 'Except that Billy might lose his life in the process. For God's sake – he's only a boy! And he's entrusted to our care! How can we possibly allow him to face that monstrosity lurking out there?'

All eyes went to Billy. He felt numb, as the professor continued with absolute calmness.

'Billy is a very special boy. No one, not even Billy, realises just how special he is. I promise you that, very soon, Billy will take the battle to his enemy and prove a formidable adversary.'

Another stunned silence swept around the table as the professor's words hit home.

This time, Becky was the first to speak up. 'When, exactly, will this *battle*, or whatever you want to call it, take place?'

The lamp brightened a little and flickered as the professor looked across at her. Billy thought that the professor's face looked increasingly vampire-like in the lamplight.

'I don't know exactly when, but I can tell you that the

Bonebreaker's spirit is very close. You can feel it, can't you, Billy?'

Billy was in no position to argue.

He felt really strange . . . tense . . . his nerves all on edge — as if something awful was about to happen. He nodded and glanced around at the anxious faces. 'It feels like he's here,' Billy found himself saying, 'right here in the room.'

Becky yelled across the table, 'Billy! You're really starting to freak me out!'

'Can you *really* feel his presence, Billy?' Mrs Truelove asked, clasping her mug of chocolate firmly to her chest.

Billy nodded gravely.

'Will you all please link hands around the table?' the professor asked, his eyes scanning nervously around the room. 'We need to concentrate and combine our psychic energy.'

The lamp began to flicker again. Everyone did as he said.

'Wow! This is turning out to be some holiday,' Calum whispered. 'It grows weirder by the minute.'

'Dad, I really don't like this,' Becky complained. 'Sam's starting to get upset. Can't we just get in the car and drive away from here?'

The professor's eyes flashed again as he looked towards her. 'Believe me, we are all being held here and we have no choice but to stand up to the evil closing in on us.'

Becky pulled her hands free and jumped to her feet. 'Well

you might say we have no choice, but some of us might think otherwise. Sam and I have had just about enough! This so-called holiday is turning into a joke – like one of those stupid old horror films you see on TV. Well I don't believe any of it! Me and Sam are going to sit in the car and listen to the radio. Give me the keys, Dad!'

As Becky stretched out her hand towards her father, the kerosene lamp spluttered and went out completely. And then the candles snuffed out, plunging the room into complete darkness. At the same time, a deafening splintering thud sounded from the centre of the table.

Becky and Sam screamed.

Almost as quickly, the lamp brightened again and everyone gasped in disbelief. Billy's eyes almost popped out of his head.

There, at the centre of the table, a fearsome battle-axe stuck out in front of them, its lethal blade embedded in the wood and its long handle angled upwards towards the ceiling.

20
Reality Check

'Don't panic!' the professor said calmly. 'Just sit down, close your eyes and link hands with the person next to you.'

Without question, everyone did as he said.

'Everything that you've just seen is in your mind,' the professor continued in a loud voice, 'planted there by the Bonebreaker. Just concentrate, try to relax and open your eyes when I count to three. One . . . two . . . three!'

Like the others, Billy did as he was told. When he opened his eyes, the axe had gone. The table was back to normal – not even a scratch mark where the axe had struck into the wood.

'Wow! That is so cool,' Calum whispered in Billy's ear.

Billy wasn't sure that 'cool' was exactly the right word to use, but no one could deny that the proceedings were spectacular.

'It's not over yet,' the professor said, as the light dimmed again.

As if to confirm his theory, Becky suddenly screamed. She stared over Sam's shoulder, her eyes wide with horror. Still linking hands, everyone turned and stared in the same direction.

A huge shadow had appeared on the wall by the steps to the trapdoor. It stretched almost to the ceiling. At first, it just stood there – a perfectly formed silhouette of the giant Viking, complete with helmet, sword in one hand and the severed head swinging from the other. And then it began to move around the octagonal walls, slowly and menacingly.

'*It's not real*,' the professor whispered loudly. 'If you're frightened, close your eyes again.'

Billy watched Becky and Mrs Truelove close their eyes tight shut. Everyone else, including Sam – much to his surprise – kept their eyes on the shadow as it glided around the walls.

'It's the same ghost we saw down by the fen,' Calum whispered across to his father.

Mr Truelove didn't reply. He stared at the spectre with a look of total disbelief. And then his expression turned to horror as the shadow reached a window and began to glide across the wooden floor towards the table. '*Professor! Do something!*' he pleaded in panic.

Sam began to sob hysterically.

'Close your eyes and trust me.' And saying this, the professor began chanting some strange words.

As the shadow reached the table, Billy let go of Calum's hand, stood up and thumped the table with all his might. 'LEAVE US ALONE!' he yelled at the top of his voice.

The result was dramatic!

The lamp went out and once again the room was plunged into darkness.

And then, almost as quickly, the power returned and the lights came on. The room flooded with light and once more everyone gasped at the scene in front of them.

There on the table were a number of small shiny stones – arranged in a pattern, as if someone had laid them there. And each of the stones was inscribed with a strange symbol.

The professor stared at them intently as he spoke. 'Keep holding hands! Focus on the stones – they contain a message.'

After a few more seconds, the professor freed his hands and reached into the inside pocket of his jacket. Billy watched in amazement as the stones vanished into thin air. Everything was normal again. It was like a dream.

Without speaking, the professor scribbled frantically in his notebook.

'What's going on, Professor?' Mr Truelove asked.

'Rune stones, Mr Truelove. Ancient stones used to convey messages – sometimes a portal to the future.'

'Has the monster gone?' Becky asked, her voice trembling with emotion.

All heads turned to the professor. 'Yes – he's gone.'

Billy sensed the enormous wave of relief that swept through the room. Mrs Truelove went to the sink and ran herself a glass of water. Becky and Sam followed her example. The professor continued to scribble on his notepad. Mr Truelove put the kettle on and suggested that they all move up to the sitting room to the warmth of the wood-burning stove.

Half an hour later, the stove was throwing out some welcome heat (the temperature in the windmill had dropped considerably) and everyone gathered around the professor.

The children sipped mugs of chocolate, whilst Mr and Mrs Truelove and the professor went in for something a good deal stronger.

'Well, what do you make of it, Professor?' Mr Truelove asked.

Professor Fenn took a sip of his whisky and looked into space. 'I've been to a number of séances and been present at all sorts of rituals over the years, but I've never witnessed anything quite so dramatic. We are indeed dealing with powerful forces.'

'No one can disagree with that,' Mrs Truelove added. 'And to think that we all thought Billy and Calum were making the whole thing up.'

'We must pull together and help Billy,' the professor

stated firmly. 'He's going to need all our support in facing up to this demon.'

Becky looked over to Billy with an expression of guilt. 'Sorry, Billy! Sam and me, we'll do anything we can to help. We promise not to tease you any more, don't we, Sam?'

Sam nodded, but said nothing – Billy sensed she was still in a state of shock.

'What about the stones?' Calum asked. 'What was the message?'

'I don't really understand it,' the professor frowned. 'It's like some sort of riddle.'

'And when you were speaking in that strange language, Professor?' Mr Truelove enquired. 'What were you saying?'

The professor placed his hands behind his head and reclined back. 'Danish – an ancient Danish dialect spoken by the Vikings. I was enquiring of the Bonebreaker when he and Billy were likely to meet – to sort out their differences, if you get my meaning?'

'And what did he say?'

'You were there, Mr Truelove. The reply was quite clear – the sudden appearance of the rune stones.'

Billy fidgeted nervously on the rug. 'But can you work out what they say?'

The professor stared at the strange symbols he'd drawn on his pad. He placed it in front of Billy. 'I've studied rune stones for years, but this arrangement is difficult to decipher. I see something divided into four equal parts.'

The professor scratched his chin and tapped the point of his pencil on the paper. 'I really need to think about this.'

'I saw the number eight hundred and sixty-five back at school. It seemed important, but I didn't know why.'

The professor turned and looked at Billy. His eyes blazed with interest and curiosity. 'Fascinating! That's when the Vikings struck East Anglia – 865.'

Billy explained again about the drawing in the art lesson – the way he'd been guided to draw the Bonebreaker's helmet.

'The knowledge is inherent in you, Billy – and perhaps some sort of spiritual communication between you and your ancestors, especially as your destiny began to draw closer.'

'Is Billy's destiny really that close, Professor?' Calum asked, his voice full of concern.

'My mum seems to think so,' Billy said. 'She sounded really worried on the phone. She said something about phases and the moon.'

The professor tapped his pencil on his notepad again. *'That's it! That's the message!'* He thrust the notepad under Billy's nose. 'These stones are arranged to match the four phases of the moon.'

They all gathered around the professor and peered over his shoulder.

'You see this last row of three stones? It represents the final phase.'

Billy couldn't see anything other than a row of strange symbols. 'Does that mean it's a full moon?' he asked.

'Exactly!' the professor replied.

Becky rushed over to the window and looked out. 'I can't see anything.'

Sam looked out of the window on the opposite wall. 'Maybe it's cloudy,' she said. 'I can't see any stars either.'

Mrs Truelove rooted through her handbag and produced a small diary. The professor watched her intently – he knew what she was doing.

'Oh my goodness!' she exclaimed, evidently finding what she was looking for. 'It's tonight – the full moon.'

Calum's parents looked across at each other. 'Look! Why don't you stay here tonight, Professor?' Mr Truelove said. 'I think we'd all feel a little safer if you did.'

Billy looked at him, hoping he would agree.

'I'm sorry . . . I have to return to the Grange – things to do. But rest assured that I shall return as soon as possible. I have Billy's interest at heart.'

Billy felt his heart sink. The professor was the only one who seemed capable of dealing with his predicament. He felt safer, less vulnerable when he was around.

'I shall take my leave now. As I said, there are things to do – least of all to try and work out how best to help. In the meantime, keep a close eye on Billy and phone me should anything more untoward happen.' And saying this, the professor wished his goodnights and disappeared through the door.

A new silence filled the room. Billy sensed he wasn't the

only one who felt vulnerable without the professor around.

'So what do we do now?' Calum asked, breaking the silence.

'We turn in,' his father answered. 'Well, at least you lot turn in. I'm going to sit up in a chair all night – keep an eye on things. I'll have the phone right by me.'

Billy started to feel faint again. His stomach filled with butterflies and he felt sick.

'Billy! You look dreadful!' Mrs Truelove cried out, getting up and walking over to him. 'Let's have you upstairs. You and Calum can sleep in our room tonight. I'll sleep here on the sofa.'

'And I'll sleep down in the kitchen,' Mr Truelove added. 'That way, we'll be spread right through the house.'

Ten minutes later, Billy almost collapsed on to the big double bed. Calum sat by his side and chatted on excitedly, going on and on about all the strange events that had taken place since the beginning of the holiday. Billy felt incredibly weak and didn't even have the strength to answer.

Calum carried on, happy to do all the talking.

Billy laid his head on the pillow and Calum's voice grew fainter and more distant as he drifted into sleep.

He slept deeply – no dreams, no nightmares, just all-enveloping blackness.

He slept through until the early hours and then awoke – he needed the loo.

He slid quietly out of bed and saw Calum gently snoring beneath the duvet.

Moonlight streamed in through a small window. Billy looked out and saw the yellow orb sitting in the starlit sky – it looked big and complete. As his feet struck the cold floor-tiles of the en-suite bathroom, he looked into the full-length mirror and jumped back at the sight of his ghostly reflection.

His hair stuck out in all directions and his eyes stared back widely from his pale face. His skin looked white and his overall appearance was zombie-like. He definitely didn't look well. No wonder Mrs Truelove had been concerned.

As he continued to stare at his spooky reflection, he thought he saw something in the mirror standing behind him. He swung round, but there was no one there.

He felt a sudden chill as the coldness of the room struck home.

He turned away from the mirror and made his way over to the toilet. As he relieved himself, he yearned for the security and warmth of his bed. But he couldn't resist glancing in the mirror again on his way back.

Once again, he found himself staring at his spooky reflection – and once again, something seemed to move behind him. He walked out of the bathroom door and deliberately jumped back, looking quickly into the glass, trying to catch out his reflection – just like the game he used to play when he was younger. But, of course, only his reflection stared back, spookier than before, the glass capturing the strange look on his face.

He felt stupid and walked over to the bed.

But as he pulled back the duvet, he felt an uncontrollable urge to go back and sneak a final look in the mirror. As Calum snored on, he crept back and peered around the edge of the door into the glass.

Horror!

The face staring back at him wasn't his. It was very similar, but somehow different.

He closed his eyes and told himself he was still in bed, dreaming. He opened them again and moved directly in front of the mirror.

His heart began to race.

There, staring back was himself in fancy dress. At least that's what it looked like. It was *his* face, but with long hair down to his shoulders. It was *his* body, but wearing some kind of woollen tunic, legs bare from the knees down and a pair of rough sandals on his feet. He looked at the face. It seemed somehow stronger than his own – the eyes more piercing, the expression more resolved.

As Billy continued to stare, the strange reflection began to speak. At least it looked as if it was speaking – its mouth began to move. But the voice sounded in Billy's head. 'My name is Wilfrid. I have waited for this moment for a very long time.'

Sensing the image wasn't hostile in any way, Billy relaxed a little. 'For which moment?'

'The moment when you and I become one.'

'What do you mean?'

'I mean the moment when the gap between us is closed.'

Billy felt a sudden chill. Goosebumps spread across his skin.

'I don't know what you mean! What gap?'

The image in the mirror glowed brighter behind the glass. 'The gap of the years between us! When the moon is complete, we shall become one and face our enemy.'

Billy gulped. *The message in the rune stones!*

Sensing that something mind-boggling was about to happen, Billy stared hard into the glass and asked the inevitable question: 'Isn't the moon already full?'

'At the end of the sixth hour the cycle will be complete.'

Billy thought for a moment and then remembered the electronic clock on the bedside table. He hardly dared look at it.

Slowly, he turned and saw the bright-red figures of the liquid crystal display. His heart froze – 5:59!

Billy braced himself . . . He couldn't begin to imagine what was going to happen next!

21
Two in One

Billy's eyes flashed from the clock back to the mirror.

'Don't be afraid, Billy!' his reflection reassured him. 'As the time arrives, I shall step into your dimension to join you. Together we will be strong.'

Billy looked back at the clock – the digits flickered to 6:00.

The image in the mirror glowed brighter and brighter. Billy shielded his eyes and was just able to see the figure step out of the glass towards him – and then it was gone.

'Wow! I must be dreaming!' Calum mumbled, sitting up in bed.

'That's what I thought,' Billy said, turning to face him. 'But it's no dream. Something's really happening. I'm feeling stronger every second!'

Billy stood there, completely mesmerised, as a radiant

glow spread through his body. His muscles seemed to tense and surge with a power he hadn't before experienced.

Finally, Wilfrid's voice spoke in his head: 'It is done! We are one! There is little time to waste. We must go to the marshes.'

Billy looked back at his reflection. It was back to normal, himself again – except he didn't look pale and weak any more. His complexion had more colour; his stature was more upright and his face had taken on a firmer expression – a look of pure resolve, similar to the one he'd seen in Wilfrid's face.

He walked over to the bunks and quickly dressed. Calum flung his duvet cover back and sat on the edge of the bed.

'Billy! What's going on?'

'We're going out … I mean, *I'm* going out – to face the demon, the Bonebreaker.'

'Did I really see someone come out of the mirror?'

Billy sat by Calum's side and pulled his socks on. 'Yes! That was me – at least me a long time ago, when my people were wiped out.'

Billy saw by Calum's face that he was struggling to understand.

'Billy, I'm not sure I know what you're talking about – but I'm coming with you!'

Billy didn't argue – he needed all the help he could get.

* * *

A few minutes later, the two of them crept down the wooden stairway, through the sitting room where Mrs Truelove slept soundly on the sofa, and out through the kitchen. They passed Mr Truelove snoring in a big chair by the telephone.

'So much for keeping watch!' Calum whispered to Billy.

A few seconds later, they stepped out into the crisp early-morning air and Billy stared up at the huge sails of the windmill. The top two sails stood out against the cold, clear sky, pointing up at the stars as they faded in the first light of dawn.

'So where do we go?' Calum asked.

Billy didn't answer. He was too busy staring up at the sinister black shape emerging from the hole in the domed roof. A loud flapping noise sounded above their heads, and Billy and Calum watched nervously as the big bird took off into the air and soared upwards. It hovered directly above them and uttered a bloodcurdling cry that rang across the sky. And then it headed off over the marshes and disappeared.

'The raven!' Calum exclaimed.

'Skallagrim!' Wilfrid spoke in Billy's head. 'He's gone to tell the Bonebreaker that we're on our way!'

'So where do we go?' Calum asked for the second time.

Billy closed his eyes, as if deep in thought. Wilfrid's voice replied to the question: 'We must go to the place you call Demon's Dyke, to the spot where you and Calum hunted for fish. We will wait there, hidden amongst the reeds.'

But what will happen after that? Billy asked himself. *If the Bonebreaker appears, it will still be a case of David versus Goliath.* Billy felt his stomach tighten again.

'Be brave!' the voice inside his head told him. 'Together, we are strong and we can defeat him.'

A short while later, Billy and Calum kept low as they walked through a field of sheep towards the reed-fringed Demon's Dyke. The sheep ignored them and grazed on the dewy grass. When Billy reached the side of the dyke, he beckoned Calum to crouch by his side amongst the reeds.

'Now what?' Calum asked nervously.

'Now we wait.'

'Billy – I'm scared!'

Billy had never heard Calum admit to being scared before.

'You're not the only one,' Billy replied. 'But Wilfrid – my other self – is confident we can beat him.'

Calum shuffled restlessly on his haunches. 'I'm glad somebody's confident. I just keep thinking about the size of that Viking. He must be as strong as an elephant.'

The reeds by their side rustled, and both Billy and Calum froze. But it was just a small bird, a reed bunting, darting amongst the thick reed-stems.

'Phew!' Calum sighed. 'I don't think I can take much more of this!'

Now something sounded behind them and on turning round, Billy watched nervously as the sheep stopped grazing and moved over towards the back of the field. They gathered in the farthest corner away from the dyke.

The voice in Billy's head confirmed his worst thoughts: 'He is coming! The animals sense it. Be ready!'

'Billy! How are we going to fight? Calum asked, his voice full of desperation. 'We haven't even got a weapon.'

'Brains and wits, that's all we need!' Billy answered. 'The rest is up to fate – and I've got this gut feeling that "payback time" is definitely on the cards.'

'I hope you're right!'

For the next few minutes they crouched in silence looking over the water towards the far bank. A pair of coots bobbed in and out of the forest of reed-stems, and then a single tiny chick appeared and swam close to its parents. It offered a pleasing distraction from the impending terror.

'Brilliant!' Billy smiled, as they watched the tiny bird swim around in circles. 'But I wonder why there's only one chick.'

The expressions on the two friends' faces turned to horror as a huge head suddenly appeared from below the watery surface. Two jaws full of razor-teeth took the tiny bird in one fell swoop and then it was gone – the parents left swimming around in helpless desperation.

'What was that?' Billy gasped.

'A pike!' Calum answered. 'A huge pike! Did you see the size of its head?'

Billy and Calum started to shake. It was as if they'd been given a sign – the Bonebreaker was surely a big pike and Calum and Billy were small chicks!

'Stay calm.' Wilfrid's voice sounded in Billy's head again. 'We can defeat the warrior, just as I defeated the great fish during my own lifetime.' An image of Wilfrid standing in a stream aiming his spear suddenly flashed into Billy's mind.

But Calum began to panic. 'Billy, we can't do this on our own. We need help. I'm going to get Dad!'

Billy remained motionless and looked up at the sky, as the raven hovered high above them. 'Please yourself! I'm staying here. I've got to do this, Calum.'

'I'll be back before you know it. Just watch yourself, Billy.'

Calum rose to his feet and headed back across the sheep field.

Billy crouched alone – but not fully alone! He sensed Wilfrid's presence. The Saxon boy was part of him and experiencing all that was happening to him. Any time now, the Bonebreaker would appear and they would face him together.

He took a deep breath and listened to the sound of Calum's fading footsteps. Calum had acted sensibly – he wasn't a coward, and he was right: they should at least have something to use as a weapon to defend themselves.

It was then that Billy saw the forked metal rod-rest sticking out of the mud. It was almost camouflaged amongst the reed-stems, and Mr Truelove must have overlooked it when they'd collected the fishing gear the previous day. He plucked it from the ground and gazed at its sharp point. Just as he was thinking that it could be used as a weapon, the reeds began to crack and rustle by his side. This time the sound was too loud to be made by a small bird. Something heavy was moving towards him.

'Ready yourself,' the voice in his head ordered. 'He is close!'

Billy turned on his haunches and stared in the direction of the sound, desperately trying to see through the thick tangle of vegetation.

The cracking, crunching noise grew louder – and then all went silent. A shiver ran down Billy's spine as he realised he was being watched. He moved his head closer towards the dense reeds and peered into them. To his horror, he saw two beady black eyes staring back.

Billy reeled backwards and dropped the rod-rest as the huge bird dived out and went straight for his eyes with its razor-beak. But he quickly recovered, spread his arms in front of his face and struggled to his feet. The bird stabbed at his forearms with incredible ferocity and immediately drew blood.

'Billy! Use your weapon!' the voice inside his head screamed.

Billy didn't understand. *What weapon?*

'The forked stick!'

Still shielding his eyes, he managed to reach down and pick up the rod-rest.

The bird shrieked hideously as Billy struggled to raise the heavy metal stick above his head. As the raven's beak struck his temple, Billy felt a searing pain and collapsed backwards again. At the same time, he instinctively let fly with the rod-rest and gave the bird a blow to its wing, so that it fell back amongst the reeds from where it had appeared.

Billy lay dazed and looked across helplessly at his attacker. The bird too, momentarily stunned, glowered back and righted itself, ready to resume its attack.

Billy leapt to his feet and raised his weapon again – but this time he never got chance to use it.

As the great bird fluttered upwards and screeched in anger, a huge axe-blade descended from somewhere above the reeds and took off its head in one sweeping blow.

Billy couldn't believe his eyes. His brain swirled in confusion as a mass of black feathers descended all around him.

'I don't think Skallagrim will bother us again!' the tall figure said calmly, as it stepped out from the reeds.

Billy wanted to run over and hug Titus Fenn, but he suddenly felt stupid, standing there – his arms bleeding and covered in mud.

'Now, young man, I think it's time we planned our next move. The Bonebreaker has no doubt been alerted to your whereabouts and is moving towards us.'

Billy smiled and felt a renewed confidence as he and the professor sat side by side and planned the next stage of their battle.

Meanwhile, just a few hundred metres upstream, the Bonebreaker was heading in their direction. He waded along the edge of the reeds, his helmet, chain mail and mighty sword reflected in the murky waters of the dyke. Soon, his lust for evil would be satisfied. Billy, the professor and any other living beings he encountered would be mercilessly slain — butchered and dispatched for the rest of eternity!

22
Time Slip

Though daylight had fully dawned, it faded against the darkening sky. An ominous bank of black clouds rolled in and the vast marshland area paled under its shadow.

Billy and the professor looked at each other. Both sensed the moment had almost arrived. The Bonebreaker was very close.

Whilst the professor rooted through his black bag and took out some stout metal pegs and tripwire, Billy related the strange business of the mirror, and how his 'other self' had somehow joined up with him. Much to his amazement, the professor didn't seem surprised. He simply nodded and carried on with his work. It was as if he'd known all along that these strange events were going to happen. Billy began to wonder if the professor was real . . . Perhaps he was some sort of ghost, like the Fen Phantom? But the dull thud of the hammer ramming the pegs deep into the soft mud sounded real enough!

'There!' the professor panted, wiping his brow on the sleeve of his coat. 'Simple, but effective! Tripwires have been used with deadly effect since the dawn of man.'

Billy went over and inspected the professor's work. The tripwire was set on the edge of the reeds – the spot where the great bird had emerged. It stretched from the waterside approximately three metres up the bank, a little way above the ground.

'As you can see, Billy, the wire is partially hidden by the reeds. As soon as the demon sees you and runs into the clearing, he's sure to strike it.'

'But will it be strong enough?' Billy asked, reaching down to feel the wire.

'It's made of steel . . . even stronger than he is. He just needs to be lured towards it.'

The professor delved back into his bag as Billy asked his next question. 'How can we be sure he'll be running?'

'By using this!' The professor took out an enormous curved horn and handed it to Billy. 'It's a Berserker war horn. It heralded the start of a raid – a massacre. When it sounded, the Vikings went literally "berserk". As soon as the Bonebreaker hears it, he'll start running. Trust me!'

Billy examined the horn. It was made out of bone – like a tusk from some sort of animal. He put it to his lips.

'Not yet, Billy!' the professor exclaimed. 'I'll signal to you when the time is right.'

'Are you sure I'll be able to blow it?'

It was the voice in his head that answered: 'I will help you.'

Billy looked back to the professor. 'And what happens if the plan works and he trips over? It's hardly going to finish him off.'

The professor picked up the huge battle-axe from in the reeds where he'd left it. He dipped the bloodied blade into the water and cleaned it with a cloth as he spoke.

'Leave the rest to me, Billy. This axe is capable of dealing with much bigger creatures than the raven. I'll hide in the bulrushes, upstream. Waiting to strike.'

Billy cringed.

He was to be the bait — the cheese in the mousetrap. The professor's dreaded battle-axe would be the instrument of death!

'OK, Saxon avenger! The trap is set. The time for battle has arrived. Stand tall and await the approach of the enemy.' And saying this, the professor took the lethal weapon and walked deep into a large patch of bulrushes, just upstream from the tripwire.

Billy watched as the professor's upper body faded into the tall stems, finally disappearing as he squatted down into a hiding position.

Although there was only a short distance between them, not being able to see the professor made Billy feel very vulnerable.

'So now I suppose I just wait,' Billy said to himself.

'But not for long,' the voice in his head replied. 'The Viking is almost upon us. I can sense the approaching power of evil. Have the horn ready.'

Billy's heart began to beat faster. He too could sense the presence drawing nearer. All around, the reeds began to crack and sway from side to side, just as on their dreaded fishing expedition, only this time on the nearside of the dyke.

The sky had grown blacker and, without warning, a discharge of raindrops splattered the mirrored surface of the dyke. At the same time, the wind sprang up, catching Billy off-guard. It was almost as if the weather had joined forces with his enemy and launched a surprise attack.

Billy stood on tiptoe, peering upstream, looking for any sign of the Bonebreaker. He shivered, half in fright and half with the cold. The rain began to drive in. The tension was unbelievable.

And then...

Somewhere just up ahead, in the direction where the professor lay hidden, a high-pitched scream rang out that chilled Billy from his head to his toes. He funnelled his hands around his mouth and cried out into the driving rain. 'Professor! Are you OK?'

The reply was a thunderous booming roar in a strange language that Billy didn't understand.

The voice in his head screamed into his brain, 'THE WARRIOR! HE'S HERE!'

Billy stared in horror as the huge figure emerged from the reeds about ten metres in front. It stood as a silhouette against the storm-filled sky, but it was easy to make out the massive frame of the Bonebreaker. Worse still, it was easy to see the helpless form of the professor being held upside down – the warrior grasping his ankle in one colossal hand and dangling him like a rag-doll.

As Billy put the horn to his lips, a sickening crack sounded across the marsh. He knew at once that it was the professor's leg being snapped. An agonising scream followed – and Billy blew the horn for all he was worth.

At first no sound came out. But the voice in his head encouraged him to try again. The second attempt worked and a deep mournful note echoed through the sodden air.

The response was dramatic.

Billy lowered the horn and gawped as the terrifying figure dropped the professor's writhing body and charged towards him. The reeds shook violently and swayed as if trying to get out of the Bonebreaker's way. Billy stood rooted to the spot – frozen like a rabbit caught in a car headlight.

His inner-self jolted him back to his senses. 'RUN! DRAW HIM TO THE TRAP!'

As his enemy's feet pounded across the marshy ground, Billy turned and headed down the side of the dyke. All the time, the rain grew faster, incessant, sweeping down in torrents. As the storm closed in, Billy began to lose his sense of direction. The dawn light had almost faded back to night.

Panicky thoughts raced through his head. *Surely the giant must have reached the tripwire by now!*

Billy finally plucked up the courage to stop and look back.

The Fen Phantom was nowhere to be seen!

He strained his eyes, peering through the rain back towards the clearing, up by the tripwire, but there was no sign of anyone.

Billy swivelled round through a complete circle, glancing in every direction. Still no sign of the Bonebreaker . . . *Where was he?*

Billy's vision suddenly blurred.

The dyke by his side disappeared – a vast expansive featureless marsh in its place. Something really weird was happening. The air filled with strange smells, unusual sounds – *and screams.*

What was happening?

Billy's head ached with confusion and his stomach churned.

'We're in my time now, Billy. We've run into the village.' As Wilfrid spoke in his head, Billy felt his body surge with renewed energy. He began to run towards the centre of the chaos, towards where the screams sounded loudest. He knew instinctively where to find his ancestral mother and sister.

Running on, he felt the coldness of the rain and the mud splattering his bare legs. He looked down and saw that he was wearing different clothes – the same rough clothes he'd seen his image wearing earlier in the mirror.

'Please tell me! What's going on?'

Running headlong into the enveloping chaos, he listened to Wilfrid's voice. 'All is happening again – as it did on the day of my mother's death. But through you, Billy, I have been given a chance to avenge the evil one.'

Billy – or was he Wilfrid – ran on, the surrounding scene becoming more horrific by the minute.

People fled in all directions from the Viking plunderers. Pitiful screams rang out everywhere. Women cried for help and frantically clung on to their children. An old man tripped and went sprawling across the ground; other villagers trampled over his prostrate body, desperate to get away.

The Viking warriors ploughed through them like wild animals.

Sword blades flashed and heavy axes swung through the acrid air. Blood spilled across the ground and mingled with the rain-washed mud. The raiders screamed in triumph and showed no mercy.

Billy gasped inwardly as he watched the slaughter unfold. It was the stuff of nightmares!

He veered away towards one of the huts on the far side of the village – he knew who would be waiting inside.

'Wilfrid! Thank God, you're here!'

Billy saw the woman sitting in a corner of the small living space. As he drew nearer, he saw that she was the spitting image of his mother. She had a young child sitting on her knee – the image of Beth.

Billy's ancestor spoke through his own voice. 'I'm here to protect you, Mother,' he heard himself saying.

'There's little you can do, Wilfrid. The devil himself is out there. Come and crouch by me.'

As Billy tried to take in all that was happening, he became aware that the screams were slowly fading outside. The massacre was obviously drawing towards its bloody end. Perhaps they would be spared after all.

But his other self knew different!

'If we do not act, Billy, they will come and take us away as slaves. And then the demon giant will kill my mother and hunt us down. But fate has given us a second chance – this time we must destroy the Bonebreaker.'

Billy tried to take it all in.

A few weeks ago he had been sat by the Forge Pond fishing with Calum, and caught his first fish. It had been wonderful – not a care in the world!

Who would have believed that such an incredible turn of events could have led to the position he was in now – trapped inside a Saxon hut … in someone else's body … a bloody massacre taking place right outside the door … about to be discovered by the most feared warrior that ever walked.

No one would believe it!

No one could believe it – because it isn't really happening, Billy tried to tell himself. *This has got to be a nightmare! It has to be!*

Just as Billy had almost convinced himself it really was all a dream, Wilfrid's little sister stirred in her mother's arms and began to cry loudly. Worse still, the more that her mother tried to comfort her, the louder she cried.

Billy looked in horror towards the door.

His heart almost stopped beating as he heard the dreaded heavy footsteps, the ensuing silence, and finally the inhuman roar of the Viking monster.

'He's here, Billy!' Wilfrid's voice trembled in his head. 'This is the moment – the time when we must face the Bonebreaker!'

23
Lethal Weapons

'Alas, Wilfrid! We are doomed! The Viking demon is about to find us. Have mercy on our souls!'

Billy looked into the sightless eyes of his ancestral mother. *But he was having none of it!*

His practical nature suddenly took over.

He looked around the small living space and saw the pointed knife lying on the wooden plate by the bread. He picked it up.

'Stay silent!' he ordered the woman by his side. 'Try to keep Beth – I mean Matilda, quiet.'

Much to Billy's relief, went all quiet and Matilda stopped crying. He swallowed hard, squatted by the side of the door and prepared to strike.

'Whatever happens next, just stay where you are and keep quiet – wait until they're gone. They might not return.'

Everyone held their breath as the huge shape approached the entrance.

As the stooping form moved through the doorway, planting one of his enormous feet just inside, Billy raised his right arm high above his head. With the combined determination of Wilfrid and himself, he brought the knife down with savage force, plunging it deep into the Bonebreaker's foot. The crouching hulk instinctively straightened up and roared like an angry bull, his huge frame instantly demolishing the doorway.

This provided the distraction that Billy needed.

He shot through the Bonebreaker's legs and charged outside into the chaos, darting amongst the startled raiders and heading towards the edge of the village.

Looking back, he saw that several Vikings were already in pursuit; the Bonebreaker close behind, limping slightly, but recovering with every determined step. But at least Wilfrid's blind mother and her daughter seemed temporarily forgotten – all eyes on Billy!

'You are indeed a great warrior,' Wilfrid's voice complimented him from somewhere in his mind. 'What shall be our next move?'

To run like hell! Billy answered. *God knows what we're going to do next!*

Glancing back again, he saw his dreaded enemy charging after him, flanked by two other Vikings and gaining fast.

He watched in disbelief as the Bonebreaker axed one of

his own men running by his side, the victim's body falling heavily in a bloody heap. The Viking running on his other flank thought better of it and veered away.

So now there were only Billy and his pursuer – and Wilfrid, of course, speaking calmly inside his head.

'Head towards the Great Marsh,' Wilfrid instructed. 'It may slow him down. His weight will not favour with the soft ground.'

Good thinking! Billy agreed.

As Billy neared the vast expanse of the marsh, the storm moved directly overhead. An intense flash of lightning struck the ground in front of him and a deafening clap of thunder followed. The ground seemed to shake and Billy stumbled and fell over, landing on his face in the squelching mud.

'Quick! Billy! Get up!' Wilfrid screamed at him. 'Our enemy is almost upon us.'

But as Billy tried to roll over, a searing pain shot through his right hand. The Bonebreaker was already upon him!

Billy looked up helplessly as the Bonebreaker stamped his wounded foot down on his hand, forcing it deep into the soft mud. Rolling further on to his back, Billy stared up helplessly at the familiar helmet – the one he'd drawn so accurately in the art lesson: four distinct bronzed panels and the letter 'S' stamped on its crown. It looked terrifying, and it was easy to imagine the real evil contained behind the blackness of the hollowed eye slits.

As he lay there, Wilfrid's thoughts echoed his own. 'Billy,

you have tried hard but fate seems to have dealt us a second blow.'

As the Bonebreaker roared and raised his mighty sword above his head, Billy closed his eyes, thought of his mum and Beth, and prepared for the moment he never really believed would happen – *the end of his short life!*

Billy never saw the lightning bolt strike the point of the Bonebreaker's sword. It sent its lethal charge down the blade, through the handle into the warrior's body and down into the marshy ground.

Sensing the delay, Billy opened his eyes and watched in awe as the Bonebreaker's mighty frame keeled over and fell like a tree in a storm.

And that wasn't the only wondrous happening . . .

Billy was wearing his own clothes again: jumper, jeans and trainers.

And he felt different – like one person again. Wilfrid had gone! He was back to being plain old Billy Hardacre.

The distant village, along with the horror of the Viking invasion, had also disappeared. Only the vast space of the fenland marsh spread out before him, the modern landscape once again dotted with windmills and grazing sheep and the reed-fringed dyke over in the distance.

But the colossal body of his enemy was still there, stretched out on the ground.

Was the Bonebreaker dead, killed by a force even greater than his own – *the force of nature?*

In answer to Billy's question, the great body began to glow — *and stir!*

The monster sat up . . . his great head staring towards Billy . . . rising to his feet.

Billy jumped up and looked around, panic welling up inside. The sky was clearing — the storm moving away. The dyke was some way over to his left. He ran towards it, the Bonebreaker all the time recovering from the lightning strike that would surely have killed any normal man.

As Billy sprinted away towards the dense reeds, he looked behind and saw the glowing monstrosity racing after him. One thought kept racing through his mind: *if this is the present, then the tripwire might still be in place.*

He ran on, the giant pounding footsteps shaking the ground close behind.

He dared not turn round. He sensed his enemy was gaining.

The reeds grew thicker and Billy swept through them, the thick stems cutting at his arms and legs.

He was tiring fast. He knew he couldn't go on for much longer.

Suddenly, he spotted the clearing. He ran towards it — and exactly at the point where the reeds stopped, he leapt into the air. There wasn't time to look down. If the tripwire was still there, at least he'd managed to clear it.

In a split second he glanced down and saw the headless

carcass of the giant bird and the rod-rest lying in the mud. In the same split second there was a terrifying roar from behind, as the sound of cracking reeds and pounding footsteps suddenly gave way to an ominous pause.

The tripwire was still there and the Viking had struck it.

Billy instinctively picked up the rod-rest and turned, as the Bonebreaker's massive frame fell through the air and toppled towards him. Gripping the metal rod in both hands and holding it point upwards, Billy fell helplessly on to his back and screamed as the Bonebreaker's upper body crashed across his legs. The enormous head, still masked by the fearsome helmet, landed directly over his chest.

Billy lay trapped on the ground, hardly able to breathe under the pressure. He could only lie there, helpless, his legs numb, waiting for the Bonebreaker to finish him off.

But the giant never moved.

Billy couldn't work out what was happening – until he felt the warm oozing liquid seeping through on to his hands.

It was only then that he thought about the rod-rest.

He was still holding it, grasping it tightly from somewhere under the Viking's helmet. He craned his neck and saw the blood-soaked point sticking out above the back of the Bonebreaker's neck.

Finally, he realised the grisly truth.

This was the telling moment, when the ancient world and the modern world were united by Bethan's curse – the metal rod-rest and the Bonebreaker's neck sharing the same point in space and time . . . both real!

Sigurd the Bonebreaker was dead!

Still trapped under the huge weight of his defeated enemy, Billy lay back in a semi-conscious state.

He looked up at the clearing sky. White woolly clouds skirted across his field of vision and in their shapes he saw faces: happy faces of Saxon villagers. He saw Wilfrid's face smiling down at him . . . and then Bethan and Matilda – no longer in fear of the Bonebreaker; they looked grateful and at peace.

Billy felt the same inner peace.

Whether by design or accident, it seemed that David had finally defeated Goliath. The Bonebreaker had been laid to rest.

Billy's mind slipped into a peaceful chasm of blackness.

He awoke in the children's orthopaedic ward of the Norwich General Hospital.

'Billy-boy! You're awake!'

Billy stared in disbelief at his mum's face. And then he looked around at the other smiling faces: Mr and Mrs Truelove, Calum, Becky and Sam.

'What happened?' Billy asked, with wide eyes.

'That may well take a good time to explain,' a familiar voice replied, approaching from somewhere more distant.

Billy and his crowd of visitors all looked around as the tall stooping figure of the professor hobbled up on crutches, one of his legs in a plaster cast stretching all the way to the top of his leg.

'Professor! You're OK!' Billy beamed, raising himself up on to his elbows.

'Well I survived!' the professor beamed back at him. 'And despite everything, it seems that you did too!'

'I tried to get help, Billy,' Calum joined in, 'just as I said I would. But when I got back with Dad, we found you lying on your back with both your legs broken.'

'And the professor with one leg broken,' Mr Truelove added.

Billy's mum dabbed her eyes with her handkerchief.

'I'm so sorry I wasn't here for you, Billy. I came down on the first train I could get. I tried to phone, but I just couldn't get through again.'

'Don't worry, Mum. I'm OK now,' Billy said, desperately trying to reassure her.

'What exactly happened out there, Billy-boy?' his mum asked nervously.

Billy stared up at the ceiling. He didn't really want to think about it. It all seemed like a horrible nightmare.

'Let him rest,' the professor said, sitting in a chair by the side of the bed. 'He's been through more than you would ever believe. He'll tell all in time. Let's just say that through Billy's bravery, four spirits are finally at peace with themselves.'

'*Four* spirits?' Billy asked, his voice full of surprise. 'Does that include the Bonebreaker?'

'Yes! Even him! I like to think that the Viking has served his penance and is finally at rest.'

'So is this business finished – all over and done with?' Mrs Truelove asked, a trace of nervousness still evident in her voice.

Billy's mum laid her hand on her son's forehead and answered. 'Yes, it's all over – for the time being. I always knew that my Billy was a special boy, but I never guessed in my wildest dreams just how special.'

'What do you mean "for the time being", Mrs Hardacre?' Becky asked, helping herself to some grapes from the dish on Billy's bedside cabinet. She offered a few to Sam.

Billy's mum looked across to the professor. He gave her a knowing smile.

'It's difficult to explain,' she answered. 'Let's just say that my Billy-boy has some interesting times ahead of him – and for the good of us all.'

'You're right, Mrs Hardacre!' the professor agreed. 'Quite right! If there are any more demons out there, then they had better watch out!'

If his mum and the professor knew what they were talking about, Billy didn't have a clue. Despite the throbbing pain in both his legs, he looked across at Calum and smiled feebly.

Calum smiled back and passed him a banana.

Everyone watched as Billy drew himself up into a sitting

position. He took the banana, peeled back the skin and took a big bite.

'You look as if you're enjoying that,' Calum said. 'Does it taste good?'

Billy was hardly able to answer at first; his mouth was too full. But he finally managed to splutter: 'Brilliant!'

Epilogue

Tom Walters went over to the window of his thatched cottage and looked out towards the river. It was Thursday night. He glanced across at the grandfather clock – it was just coming up to eleven-thirty: time to turn in. But tonight he sensed a change in the air. He felt a sudden urge to put on his hat and coat and walk over to the river.

It was just before midnight when Tom saw the bright-orange glow. It was coming from somewhere upstream, just round the top bend – but it seemed to be drawing closer. He crouched among the reeds and listened to the excited voices on the far bank. He watched in awe as the strange silhouettes ploughed through the far reeds making their way downstream. The fierce warlike helmets stood out against the dark skyline.

Viking warriors!

Tom crouched as still as a heron and listened to their drunken song, in a dialect way beyond his understanding. He finally turned his head and gasped as a Viking longboat, engulfed in flames, drifted into view. The blood-red sails burnt brightly, the material disintegrating into a starburst of shimmering embers, catching on the cold night air and spiralling upwards towards the watching moon. And on the deck a dark shape stood out as it lay in the heart of the bonfire.

Tom knew at once it was him – the Fen Phantom – the Bonebreaker!

It was a funeral pyre, his corpse being offered up to Odin in the true Viking tradition. And as the warlike silhouettes continued to throng down the far bank, Tom detected the air of celebration and excitement in their voices.

And no wonder!

They were rid of the demon that walked among them – the one that claimed to be of their blood, their ally. But in truth, his own people feared him – even more than they feared Odin himself.

Tom stayed hidden, and watched until the blazing vessel finally moved out of sight downstream, the orange glow fading back into darkness.

A short while later, everything was back to normal, as if nothing untoward had happened – except that there was a peacefulness left hanging in the air.

The old man got up, rubbed the tops of his legs to

stimulate them back into action, and slowly made his way back to the warmth of his cottage.

As he climbed into bed he said a little prayer, smiled to himself, and decided that tomorrow he would dust off his fishing tackle and return to the dykes. It would be good to have a go at the pike again – something he hadn't dared to do for a long time!